UNEXPECTED LOVE ON CHRISTMAS EVE

A SECOND CHANCE ROMANCE

EMORIE COLE

KEWEENAW PUBLISHING LLC

SOPHIE

*H*orns are honking all around me as I sit in bumper to bumper traffic, waiting to escape downtown Chicago. It's almost Christmas and everyone is trying to flee the city for vacations or just heading home to be with their families after leaving work early. This time of the year the traffic is even crazier than usual, with tourists in town for the holidays and people running around to do last minute errands. I'm looking forward to getting away from it all.

This is the first Christmas that I'll be spending alone instead of with my family. My parents are vacationing in Australia this year and my sister Jessica is studying abroad in Paris. My mom and dad invited me to join them, but as a teacher my winter break wouldn't have started before they left and it will be over long before they return. Sure, I could have gone with different travel dates, but the thought of Christmas without snow just doesn't appeal to me. I envy Jessica—Paris at Christmas, I have always thought it would be beautiful, but I didn't want to interfere with her studies and her time enjoying the study abroad experience—having her big sister tagging along might put a damper on all of her fun. So I've chosen to be on my own this year.

Since I'll be by myself, I have decided to rent a cabin in my hometown of Winterglen, Michigan. My parents and sister moved to Seattle soon after I went away to college, so my childhood home is no longer an option to stay at and I don't want to impose on any of my friends that still live there. Besides, the thought of having a cozy cabin for Christmas is something that sounds wonderful. I can imagine spending peaceful nights just watching the snow falling outside, basking in the glow of the Christmas tree while the fireplace keeps me warm, and sipping a cup of hot chocolate. It will be nice to have some peace and quiet for a change.

I glance at the clock on the dashboard and sigh as I inch slowly closer towards my exit. It's already mid-afternoon and I have a couple of hours to drive. As a teacher my vacation started yesterday, but I chose to wait until today to travel so that I could finish packing without rushing. I had hoped to leave first thing this morning, but thanks to a flat tire that had to be replaced, I'm getting a later start.

It's only a couple of hours to travel from Chicago to Winterglen, so I'm driving myself there instead of flying. It'll be easier than having to rent a car. Unlike Chicago, Winterglen doesn't have all of the crazy traffic. I'm looking forward to not having to sit in the car for half-an-hour just to go a short distance.

Don't get me wrong—I love living in the city. I moved to Chicago right after college when I accepted a position as a first grade teacher. But it can get crazy during the holidays. Everyone always seems to be in a hurry to get somewhere and the malls are crammed with last minute shoppers trying to find the hottest toys or the newest electronics. Winterglen has always been the opposite. Since it is such a small town, it's never packed with traffic, shops are always busy—but not overly crowded, and everyone takes their time getting around. People will stop to visit on the streets because everyone who lives there knows everyone else and takes the time to talk with tourists, welcoming them to the town. I'm anxious to return to that small town life for a while.

The cars in front of me start moving faster and I reach my exit in a couple of minutes. Breathing a sigh of relief as I finally make it out of the city, I relax a bit as the divided highway turns into a two lane road, surrounded by nothing but trees. Traffic seems to disappear as I get farther out of the city and eventually turns to only a few cars that I pass every couple of miles—all going in the opposite direction towards Chicago. The towns that I pass through are few and far between—most having nothing except for one stoplight, a grocery store, gas station, and a handful of houses.

As I pass the sign welcoming me to Winterglen a few hours later I smile to myself. The snow is gently falling and the town looks magical with all of its decorations on the lampposts and in the store front windows. It reminds me of the joy I had here as a little girl, spending all of my Christmases with my family partaking in the small town festivities and community fun. I remember caroling with my parents, sledding with my sister, and hours of playing outside in the snow followed by hot chocolate at the diner.

I pull to a stop in front of the hardware store that is still owned by Mr. Elliott—a family friend since I was little. The owner of the cabin that I have rented, Rachel, is a friend of his as well and said that she would leave the keys for me with him at the store. I walk in and he turns around at the sound of the little bell above the door dinging.

"Sophie! How are you? It's been quite a while since you last visited," he says with a bright smile.

"Hi, Mr. Elliott. I'm doing great. It feels like forever since I was here last, but I'm looking forward to being here now for Christmas. It's my favorite time of year."

"It's my favorite time of the year too. Especially with all of the town events happening."

"Are they still having the big Christmas Eve dance? I always loved going to it when I was younger."

"Of course! Wouldn't be a proper Christmas celebration without the dance!"

I smile at him and say, "Awesome! I can't wait!"

He chuckles and asks, "Now what can I do for you, Sophie?"

"Right. Do you have some keys for me? I rented a cabin over on Renaissance Street from Rachel and she said that she would leave the keys with you."

"Ah, yes! She did mention that you would be stopping by. Let me grab them for you," he says as he heads back towards his office. While I wait I look around the shop. The old gum ball machine that I remember from my childhood still sits in the corner. The retro payphone still hangs on the wall in the back of the shop. I haven't seen one of those in years! I didn't even know they still existed.

When he returns he hands me a set of silver keys with a 'Home Sweet Home' cabin keychain attached to them. "Here you go, Sophie. It's a beautiful little cabin you are renting over there. I hope you're planning on attending some of the festivities. It would be great to see you out there around town."

"Of course! I wouldn't miss them for the world."

"I will see you later then, drive safe."

"I will. Thanks."

I leave the hardware store and get back into my car to make the short drive to the other side of town. I pass by so many places that I have fond memories of along the way that I can't help but to think that I've made a wise decision to spend my Christmas here. The drive takes me past Callie's Diner where I would go with my mom and sister on chilly mornings to grab hot chocolate, the town square where we would always go to the Christmas tree lighting and outdoor ice skating rink, and the community center where the big dance always took place.

When I pull up in front of the cabin I know that it will be perfect. It is a cozy little log cabin with a small porch attached to the front. I put my car in park and hop out to go explore the inside. I climb the two stairs to get onto the porch and put the key into the lock. Pushing the door open I walk inside to a beautiful sight. On the wall opposite the door, there are huge windows that overlook a snowy wonderland. Tall pine trees with their branches blanketed in snow stretch on for what looks like miles. There is a living room with a fireplace—I can already see myself curling up in front of a warm fire with a good book, enjoying the lights of the Christmas tree that I could place in the corner. A small kitchen and dining area complete the main area.

I wander through the doorway on my left that leads down a small hallway to the bedrooms. Depositing my bags in the first bedroom, I walk down the hall to the second bedroom. Since I will have this place all to myself I figure I may as well see which room I like the best. Both rooms seem to be the same size and have a similar feel so I decide it doesn't really matter. As I am walking back to the first bedroom I pass the door that leads to the bathroom. Just as I am about to open it, the door flies open. There—standing in nothing but a small towel wrapped around his waist—is my ex-boyfriend Matt O'Connor. "What are you doing here?" I shriek.

"Taking a shower," he replies with a smirk. "What are you doing here?" He stands there in front of me with his chiseled abs, muscles upon muscles in his shoulders and chest, and his chestnut-brown hair slightly mussed from toweling it dry. I can feel the heat flush my cheeks as my body tingles from the sight of him. I dig my fingernails into my palms to keep myself in check—my body may be responding to the sight of him, but all I really want to do is slap the jerk across his face. He broke my heart a long time ago and I am not about to let him do it again.

"This is *my* cabin for the next two weeks. That's what I'm doing here. So I'll ask you again, what are *you* doing here Matt?"

"I think you're mistaken sweetheart. This is my cabin for the next two weeks."

"What do you mean it's *your* cabin? And don't call me sweetheart! You lost that privilege when you left me and broke my heart."

He looks down at the floor before looking back up at me and says, "I'm really sorry about that Sophie. I never meant to hurt you."

"Whatever," I sputter. "Now what do you mean that this cabin is yours?"

Matt walks over to the kitchen counter and picks up his cell phone—which I hadn't seen lying there when I had first arrived. He scrolls for a minute, finds what he is looking for, and hands it to me. It is the rental agreement for the cabin, *his* rental agreement. I gasp as I see it, then pull my own cell phone out of my purse and find my email with the rental agreement that *I* had signed. "Damnit! It looks like we both rented this cabin for the next two weeks. You need to fix this! There is no way that I'm staying here with you for that long."

"You could just leave and find somewhere else to stay," Matt says.

"No way! I'm not giving up my perfect vacation spot!"

"Relax," he says, "I was just joking. We will just call the owners who rented us the cabin and see what we can do about it." He dials the number for the owners, puts it on speaker so that I can hear, and waits for them to pick up. "Hi, is this Rachel? My name is Matt O'Connor. I'm currently renting your cabin and there is a bit of a problem. It seems that I'm not the only one that you rented it to. I'm standing here with Sophie Lebeau."

"Oh, no!" Rachel says. "Hold on one second and let me check something." There is a short pause on her end of the line and we can hear hushed conversation in the background. When she comes back she says, "I'm so sorry! It would appear that my husband forgot that I had already rented to Sophie and he rented it to you, too Matt. We would be more than happy to issue a refund if one of you decides to leave —though I'm not sure if you'll find any other accommodations at this time of year. Again, I apologize for the inconvenience."

"That's alright. Let Sophie and I talk it over and I will let you know what we decide. Thanks." Matt hangs up the phone and looks at me. "Well, that explains why we both have rental agreements. Now we just need to decide what we are going to do about it."

"There's nothing to decide. You heard her—she said they would be happy to provide you with a refund when you leave."

"What do you mean me? I'm not going anywhere!"

"Well I'm not leaving either!"

"You don't understand. I have to stay here," Matt says.

"Why?" I ask.

"I just do, okay?"

"Fine. Don't tell me. Let's just look to see if we can find another hotel or rental and *then* you can leave." Taking out my laptop I open my browser and start searching for places to stay in Winterglen. After looking for what seems like hours, Matt and I come to the conclusion that there is absolutely nowhere else to stay. Everything is booked full. "Ugh, fine," I say at last. "There are two bedrooms here. You take one, I'll take the other, and we'll avoid each other as much as possible."

"Fine. That'll work," Matt says.

Gathering my laptop, my phone, and my purse I stomp down the hallway to the room I had left my bags in and slam the door shut behind me. I hear Matt grumbling something about how he likes the other room better anyway as he rolls his suitcase down the hallway. Apparently I had been so wrapped up in the beauty of the cabin that I had missed seeing any of his stuff—his phone, suitcase, and car—when I had arrived. Great, just great. Spending the next two weeks in a cabin with my ex-boyfriend is not exactly how I had planned on spending my Christmas vacation. This just became the worst Christmas vacation ever!

MATT

*A*s I drop my suitcase off into the room at the end of the hall in the cozy cabin, I can't believe my luck. At this point I'm not sure if it is good luck or bad luck. I had rented this cabin in my hometown to hide from a crazy stalker, Victoria, who has been dead-set on being my girlfriend for years, and now I am sharing the cabin with an ex-girlfriend—though, Sophie isn't crazy. Part of me wonders if this will be the perfect opportunity to try to pick up where things had left off between Sophie and I. But on the other hand I know that it won't be easy since Sophie seems to despise even the sight of me. How can I blame her, though? I had acted like a jackass and it is my fault that she is no longer a part of my life.

We had been high school sweethearts. I met Sophie when we were kids and we were friends for most of our lives before we started dating in high school. We were together all four years, sharing all of the special occasions like homecoming and prom together. The cliché couple—football quarterback and head cheerleader. Our relationship was perfect and we made plans to stay together when we went off to college, but she was accepted to her dream school in a different state and I had been accepted to the University of Michigan. Sophie assured me that she was good with a long-distance relationship, but I didn't want to hold her back. The resentment she no doubt would have felt if she missed out on the full college experience would have killed me. I wanted her to be free to go out and do whatever she wanted without feeling guilty or tied down. So I broke up with her. Looking back, I should have at least told her why I was breaking up with her instead of just telling her that I felt like it was for the best. Regardless of what happened all those years ago, I still feel like breaking up had been the biggest mistake of my life. Now that I finally have some time with her, maybe I can at least fix our friendship.

After digging some jeans and a sweater out of my suitcase I get dressed and go back to the kitchen to make something to eat. Sophie had come back out of her room and is sitting on the couch in the living room typing on her computer. "What are you working on?" I ask her.

"None of your business," she says cooly, "and we are supposed to be avoiding each other—so stop talking to me."

"Alright," I say, holding my hands up and walking backwards towards the kitchen. "I won't say another word." Sophie rolls her eyes at me before going back to whatever it is she is working on.

I open the refrigerator and pull out everything that I will need to make Chicken Parmesan. It had been one of Sophie's favorite meals when we were together. Hopefully she still likes it and I can convince her to join me. As I cook, I keep glancing over to where she is sitting and find that she keeps looking towards the kitchen. I know the aromas of the seasoned chicken and tomato sauce are getting to her. "Would you like to join me for dinner, Sophie? I made extra just for you."

"No, I'm fine." Sophie isn't convincing in her reply. I always knew that she was lying when she scrunched up her nose—like she is doing now.

"Alright. I'll just dish up this wonderful home cooked meal for myself then. Juicy chicken, pasta—"

She sighs as her stomach grumbles loudly and I chuckle. "Fine." She puts her computer down and walks over to the kitchen. She closes her eyes and sniffs the air. "Mmm….It does smell amazing. But I'm only eating because I'm starving—this doesn't change anything." She opens the cabinet to grab some cups and walks to the refrigerator to find drinks for the two of us.

"Fair enough," I say as I dish up two plates. I carry them over to the dining table and she follows me with the two glasses of water that she had poured.

Taking a bite of the food she says, "Matt, this is *delicious*. When did *you* learn how to cook?"

I smile at her. "I learned how to cook for myself when I went to college, you know. I even picked up a few recipes from my mom."

She looks sad for a minute and I wonder if maybe I shouldn't have mentioned college, but then she shakes her head as if clearing her mind and says, "I remember your mom's cooking. She used to make this meal every week for me."

We both smile fondly at the memory of those nights. Every week she would come over to my house for a movie night. My mom would cook Chicken Parmesan for dinner, we would have ice cream for dessert, and then we would grab blankets and cuddle on the couch to watch whatever movie we felt like that week. Those had always been some of my favorite memories. "We had some really good times, didn't we?" I ask her.

"Yeah—we did," she says sadly. "Matt—what happened between us? I mean, I always thought that everything was so good, so right. Then one day you just told me that we were done."

I sit quietly for a minute trying to think of the right words to explain to her why I broke up with her. "Sophie, I—nothing—ugh." I rub my hands across my face. "Nothing happened. I was an idiot. Letting you go almost killed me because I didn't want to break up with you."

"Then why did you?" Sophie looks so heartbroken and confused. But how can I blame her? I just told her that I *didn't* want to break up with her when I did all those years ago.

"Because you were accepted into your dream school and I didn't want to hold you back. I wanted you to have all of the college experiences that you could. I didn't want you to feel like you missed out on something or that you were tied down. I thought you would resent me for it later and I couldn't live with that guilt. So I had to let you go."

"Are you sure that it wasn't *you* who would have

felt tied down? That *you* weren't the one who would have hated having the long-distance relationship holding you back from all of the women and glamour that your college experience was going to provide? Thinking that I was just going to be the 'girl back home' when there were beautiful coeds hanging onto every one of your football highlights?" she asks.

"No. That never even occurred to me." I'm taken aback by her comments. Is that really what she has thought of me for the past ten years? "I never even dated anyone else for the whole first year and a half that I was there. I was still heartbroken over losing you. I thought I was doing the right thing putting you first. Looking back, letting you go has always been my biggest regret."

I can see the tears welling up in Sophie's eyes as she looks back toward me. "I have never really gotten over you either, you know. None of my other relationships even came close to what you and I had."

"Maybe we can get that back," I say cautiously.

"Matt—I may still have feelings for you, but I don't think I can ever trust you with my heart again," she says sadly.

"I understand. Really, I do. But could we at least

try to be friends again? I miss having you in my life. And if we are going to be here together for the next two weeks, it would make it more pleasant if we were actually friendly instead of avoiding each other. Don't you think?"

Sophie stands up from her chair and looks out at the snow covered trees that line the yard. She takes a deep breath as I watch her with my own breath held, hoping that she will at least let me try to rekindle our long lost friendship. "Alright," she says at last, "I think in the spirit of Christmas the least I can do is give you a second chance at being friends again."

"Great." I smile at Sophie as I push up from my chair and walk over to the freezer. Pulling out a container of chocolate ice cream I turn to her and ask, "Ready for some dessert?"

Sophie smiles and laughs. "Definitely!"

I scoop the ice cream into bowls and bring it over to the table, setting one bowl in front of Sophie and the other in front of myself. "So I saw that the town events start tomorrow night with the town tree lighting. Do you want to go?"

"Sure. But remember—just as friends," she replies as she takes a bite.

"Just as friends," I assure her.

"Great! In that case it will be fun! You know what

we should do tonight though?" she asks as she eats another spoonful of ice cream.

"What should we do?"

"We should go cut down a Christmas tree and decorate it. It would look perfect over in the corner near the fireplace."

"That sounds like a great idea. Let me clean up the dishes after we finish the ice cream and then we can go to the Christmas tree farm and choose one. We can take my truck."

"Okay. Your truck—where is it by the way? I didn't see it when I got here which is why you startled me."

"I parked it on the side of the cabin."

"I parked and came in through the front. Guess that would explain why I didn't see it."

I start laughing. "You never were all that observant. Some things never change I guess."

"Shut up," she mutters with a smirk.

When we finish eating I clean up the dishes while Sophie goes to change into something a little warmer. With the sun gone down, the temperature is dropping pretty quickly. Grabbing my thick blue winter coat, I put it on and tie my winter boots while I wait for her. Sophie comes out of her bedroom wearing the same pair of jeans that she had been wearing earlier, but with a warmer sweater. She puts on her coat and boots, grabs her hat and gloves and we head out the side door to my truck.

The tree farm that we are heading to has always been a favorite spot for the locals. The drive over is filled with pleasant conversation—sticking to friendly, *safe* topics, not mentioning anything from our past. I climb out of my truck while Sophie digs through her purse for her cell phone to respond to a text message she just received. I quickly go around to the other side and open the door for Sophie. She glances at me with a look of surprise on her face that turns into a smile. "Thank you," she says softly.

"You're welcome."

We walk over to the entrance of the farm where Sophie and I make our way down the rows of trees, searching for the perfect one. There are short trees, fat trees, tall trees, and skinny trees. Trees of all shapes and sizes. What a sight to see. "So many to choose from," I say.

"Yes, but it has to be *just right*," she replies. We finally come to one that is the perfect height and has big, bushy branches. "It's perfect!" she exclaims.

I take the axe that I had thrown into the back of my truck and start to wind up. "Do you know what you're doing with that thing?" she asks hesitantly.

"Of course I do. Who do you think helped chop all of that firewood at my parents' house when we were younger?" I swing the axe and strike the tree, watching as it topples down perfectly to the side. Sophie helps me carry it back to the parking lot and tie it down in the bed of my truck before I go to pay for it. As we are about to start making our way back to the cabin I realize that we don't have any decorations so I turn in the opposite direction and head to the hardware store.

"Where are we going? The cabin is in the other direction."

"We don't have any decorations for it. I'm going to stop at Mr. Elliott's hardware store so we can get some."

"Oh, right. I forgot that we didn't have any."

When we arrive we go inside to make our purchases.

"Hi, Matt! I see you and Sophie are together again!" Mr. Elliott says happily as he sees us walk through the door.

"Well, not *together* together, but there was a bit of a mix-up and we are both staying at the same cabin."

"Ohhh. Come to think of it, I did get keys from both Rachel and David—but it never occurred to me that the keys were for the *same* cabin. They used to have another place they would rent out, but I forgot they sold it a couple of years ago. I guess you two are making the best of it and sharing the cabin?"

"Yes, sir."

"Ohh—don't *sir* me," he says waving his hand. "Now, what can I help you with?"

"We just came in to get some decorations for a Christmas tree," Sophie says.

"Excellent! I've got plenty. Take a look around and just let me know what you two decide on."

"Thanks, Mr. Elliott," she says.

Sophie and I take our time looking around the store, browsing through the rather large collection of lights and ornaments. There are garlands in every color, lights in various shapes and sizes, and bulbs decorated with almost every design imaginable. I choose some colorful lights while Sophie chooses a variety of ornaments and blue and silver garland. After we make our final selections we pay Mr. Elliott and head out to my truck, putting the bags inside before we both climb in to make the drive back to the cabin.

Once we arrive, we haul the tree inside and set it up in the corner. "Now it's time to decorate!" Sophie says excitedly.

It is nice seeing her smile and happy like this

again. The last time I had seen her she had been so upset with me, but I can't focus on the past. I need to move forward so I push those thoughts out of my mind. "What should we do first?" I say with a smile.

"I think it would be easiest to string the lights on first, then we can hang the ornaments and lastly the garland."

"Sounds good to me." I reach for the string of lights that is in the bag on the floor. Grabbing one end, I start to slowly string them around the top of the tree, handing them to Sophie halfway around to pass back to me. We continue going back and forth until the entire tree has been decorated with the multicolored lights. Sophie pulls the boxes of ornaments and garland out of the bags. We take turns selecting ornaments and hanging them on the tree. As the tree starts to fill up with ornaments we finish it off by wrapping the colorful garland around in a similar fashion to how we hung the lights. When it is finished we both take a step back to admire our work.

"So beautiful," Sophie whispers.

"It really is," I say, looking at her and not the tree. I have always found her long blonde hair and green eyes—the color of emeralds—to be beautiful. *She* is beautiful.

As we stand here, side by side, next to the tree it is easy to forget that we broke up years ago. It feels so natural to be back together like this. It reminds me of all of the times we used to have together. She turns towards me and we look into each other's eyes. "Um—I—I'm going to go to bed. I'm really tired. Thanks again for dinner and for helping with the tree. I'll see you in the morning." She pushes a golden lock of hair behind her ear. "Goodnight, Matt."

"Goodnight, Sophie." I watch as she walks away towards her bedroom. Tonight couldn't have gone any better. Hopefully we are on the road to repairing what we had. At least she doesn't hate me anymore.

SOPHIE

Back in the safety of my bedroom I lean against the door, close my eyes, and take a deep breath. Spending the day with Matt has brought back all of those old feelings that I had pushed out of my mind years ago. I have never really gotten over Matt and all of my relationships since him have been short and uneventful. I realized a long time ago that I had always compared new relationships to what Matt and I had shared. Unfortunately nothing has ever come close to what we had.

Seeing him at the cabin had been a shock to me at first, but spending time with him again has made me feel whole again—like something has been missing until now. I can't believe that Matt still remembers my favorite foods, but when he made

Chicken Parmesan for dinner and chocolate ice cream for dessert I found myself trying to hide how happy it made me feel. Decorating the Christmas tree had also stirred up memories of when we used to decorate the trees at his parents' house and mine. We had always had such a great time doing it that it had become a yearly thing. My family had welcomed him into our yearly traditions just as his family had welcomed me into theirs. It felt like we would be together forever.

For now, I have agreed to rekindle our friendship, but that's it. I will need to be careful not to cross that line. Moving into my room, I find my pajamas in my suitcase and put them on. I get ready for bed, grab my laptop and climb into bed. Opening the laptop I respond to a few emails I had received, look up the schedule of town events to write down the few that I absolutely have to attend, then put my laptop away and turn off my light.

I drift in and out of sleep, dreaming of Matt whenever those moments of sleep come. It feels like I have been doing that for hours when I finally give up on sleeping and crawl out of bed. It's still dark outside, but looking at the clock I see that it is five A.M. I venture out into the kitchen quietly to make myself a cup of coffee. As I am waiting for the coffee maker to finish brewing I hear Matt come out into the kitchen.

"Morning," he says.

"Morning. What are you doing up so early?"

"Habit. I teach an eight A.M. class most days, so I've just gotten used to getting up early to get ready."

"You teach?" I ask.

"Yeah, I'm a professor at the University of Illinois at Chicago."

"Seriously? You live in Chicago, too?"

"What do you mean, too? Do *you* live in Chicago?"

"Yeah, I do actually. I'm a first grade teacher at an elementary school there."

"Wow. I had no idea that we've been in the same city all this time."

"Neither did I. Though, to be fair, it's probably a good thing that I didn't know you live in Chicago. Until yesterday, I haven't exactly been your biggest fan. If I had known you live in Chicago I probably would have moved just to get as far away from you as possible."

"Ouch," he grimaces. "I deserve that."

"Yes you do. Anyways, what kind of classes do you teach?" The coffee maker finishes brewing and I pour myself a cup. It smells wonderful. "Want a cup?" I ask as I am already reaching for a second cup.

"Yes please. Thank you. I'm an accounting professor. I teach mostly Intro to Accounting and second year accounting classes."

"You always did love numbers," I say as I hand him a coffee mug with little snowman feet. "It's not really surprising that you teach accounting."

"Really? Snowman feet?" Matt asks as he takes the mug. He smiles at me and chuckles. "Yeah, I guess I always did like working with numbers."

Sipping my coffee, I shuffle over to the table and take a seat. I watch as Matt walks over and sits down across from me. Since I have forgiven him enough to be friends again, I decided to invite him to do something with me today before we go to the tree lighting ceremony. "So, I was looking at the calendar of events last night before bed and it doesn't look like there is anything before the tree lighting. I was thinking it might be fun to go out to the old sledding hill. Would you want to go with me?" I ask.

Matt searches my face for a moment before answering. "You really want me to come?"

"Well….we agreed to be friends again, and sledding is more fun when you're not alone, so yeah, I really want you to come."

"Alright. I'll come, but only if we can have a sled race."

"Really? A sled race? Aren't we a little old for that?"

"Never!" Matt says with a laugh. "Besides, if we were too old for sled races wouldn't that mean we are too old for the town events we plan to go to?"

Now it is my turn to laugh. "Yeah, I guess you're right and we are definitely not too old for those." I finish my coffee and stand up to bring my cup to the sink. Matt follows behind with his mug. After washing the cups and the coffee pot, I tell Matt that I need to shower and get dressed. I head to my room to grab my clothes and walk into the bathroom to turn on the water for the shower. Getting undressed and climbing under the hot spray of water, I think about the day ahead. I can do this—I can be friends with Matt and not let myself get carried away.

Ten minutes later, I emerge from the bathroom dressed in my favorite pair of skinny jeans and a fluffy green sweater that matches my eyes. It is still early, the sun hasn't even risen yet, so I have a couple of hours until Matt and I are going to go sledding. Reaching into my suitcase, I pull out my favorite book that I had brought with me and go into the living room to read in front of the fireplace. Since the fireplace is gas or wood, it will be easy enough to flip the switch and have a cozy fire that can be easily turned off before we leave. I prefer a wood fire—the rustic smell of the logs burning and those cute colorful pinecones that make the flames dance in an array of colors makes it feel more festive—but a gas fire will have to do for now. Grabbing the extra blanket that was on my bed, I walk into the living room, flip the switch for the fire, and curl up on the couch to read.

I have been reading for quite a while when Matt finally comes into the living room. He is showered and ready for the day ahead. His face is clean shaven and his scent is the familiar sandalwood smell that I remember from all those years ago. He looks amazing in his jeans and red sweater—both show off his muscled features. He walks over to the couch and asks, "Mind if I sit here with you?"

"Not at all."

He sits down at the other end of the couch by my feet. We sit in companionable silence while I continue to read and he just enjoys the flickering fire and the sparkling lights from the tree. As I am reading, I keep getting distracted thinking about how much I have missed these moments with Matt. We had spent many nights sitting together—just being together—when we were younger. For the past ten years I hadn't had him in my life, but I had never allowed myself to think about how much I wanted him back until now. But allowing him back into my life as a friend is one thing, allowing him back in as a boyfriend is a completely different story and isn't going to happen if I can help it. He had hurt me too badly the first time. It isn't something I want to go through again.

After sitting together for some time, my stomach starts to growl and I realize that I haven't eaten since last night. "I'm starving. Should we have some breakfast before we go to the sledding hill?" I ask Matt.

"Sure. I could use some food. Especially if I'm going to beat you in the sledding race," he says with a smirk.

"In your dreams! I'm going to leave you in my dust—or snow!" I say with a laugh. We walk into the kitchen and make some pancakes for breakfast. Sitting down at the table to eat I look out the windows at the beautiful view. It snowed last night and the morning sunlight is glistening on the freshly fallen snow making it shimmer. It reminds me of looking into a snow globe filled with glitter and a wintery scene—a small town blanketed in white snow made out of glitter so that it shines when you shake it. Smiling to myself, I think of how I had always imagined Winterglen to be magical when I was little because of the beautiful, snowy winters we had. I still think it's magical.

"Hello—Earth to Sophie!" Matt says in a teasing voice.

"Huh? Oh, sorry. I guess I spaced out a little there."

"What were you thinking about?"

"I was just thinking about how I always thought this town was magical when I was little. And how I always feel like I'm living in a snow globe when I look outside."

"Yeah—I always thought there was magic in this town, too," Matt says as he takes another bite of his breakfast.

When we finish eating and cleaning up Matt asks, "Are you ready to have some fun?"

"Definitely! Let's go!"

We hurry to put on our winter gear and rush outside. We make a quick stop at the store to buy a couple of sleds and then Matt drives us to the sledding hill that we had frequented often as children. After parking the vehicle, we jump out and grab our new sleds out of the back of the truck. I am anxious to see if I can still beat him down the hill like I had in the past. He was always the slow one. "You ready, Matt?" I ask.

"Bring it on," he teases.

We hike up to the top of the hill and get into position. "On the count of three we race to the bottom."

"What does the winner get?"

"I don't know. What did you have in mind?"

"Loser buys hot chocolate at Callie's Diner."

"Deal!" I say. Callie's Diner has been the town's most popular hangout for locals for as long as I can remember. The diner always makes the best hot chocolate and I can never find anything that compares to it anywhere else. I swear it's the local, small town charm that makes it taste so good. Or maybe it's just drinking it with friends and neighbors that makes it so special. Either way it's fantastic.

"Alright then. Let's do this!" Matt says with excitement. "One….two…." He pushes himself forward and launches down the hill.

"Hey! No fair!" I yell as I give myself a push forward to try to catch up. By the time we have both reached the bottom we are both laughing. We slide to a stop just before crashing into the giant snowbank, Matt seconds before me. "Cheater!" I yell good-naturedly. "I totally would have beaten you."

"I know," he chuckles. "You always used to beat me at the sledding races. I had to win against you at least once. But since I did cheat, I will buy the hot chocolate."

"No, it's fine. I'll buy it this time. But you owe me."

"Fair enough."

We pick up our sleds and climb back to the top of the hill. It's such a beautiful day—the snow is gently falling, adding a soft powder to sled on and the sun is shining. Children are laughing and having fun as they fly down the hill on their toboggans, their parents watching them as they race. It's a busy, exciting place today. After a few more runs down we head back to the truck to go get the hot chocolate and warm up. The ride to the diner feels comfortable and familiar—we are talking and joking like we used to. It feels so natural being here with him again.

When we get to Callie's Diner we go inside and walk up to the counter to place our order. "Two hot chocolates, please," I say to the young girl behind the counter.

"She'll have hers with no whipped cream," Matt pipes in.

I smile and nod to the girl before turning to Matt. "You remember that I don't like whipped cream in mine."

"Of course I do. How could I ever forget?"

The girl rings up our order in the cash register. I hand over my credit card to pay and ask Matt to save us a table. He finds an open booth and sits down while I wait for our drinks. Taking them from the girl I say, "Thank you," and walk over to join Matt.

"Here you go," I say as I hand him his hot chocolate.

"Thank you. Next time I'll buy," he says with a smile.

"I know you will," I tease. Taking a sip of my drink I close my eyes as I enjoy the chocolatey goodness. It is thick and creamy, extra chocolate, and not too hot. It is the perfect winter treat.

As we drink our hot chocolate Callie, the owner of the diner, comes over to our table. She has worked here since she opened the diner over thirty years ago. She's a cheerful old woman with gray hair piled on top of her head and always wearing gold bangle bracelets. "My goodness," she says. "I haven't seen the two of you in ages. It's so nice to see the two of you together again. You always did make such a cute couple."

"We're not a couple," I say quickly. "Just friends now."

"Is that right?" she asks Matt.

"It is," replies Matt sadly. "Just friends." Is he really sad about being *just* friends? Even if that is the case I still can't allow it to be anything more than that between us.

"Well, I'm sure whatever changed your relationship, you two can work it out," Callie says confidently. "How are your drinks?"

"Excellent, as always!" I say. "What makes the hot chocolate taste *so* good?"

"My secret ingredient—it's made with love," Callie says with a wink. "Well, I better be checking in with everyone else. It was good to see both of you again." With a quick wave she saunters away to visit with the customers at all of the other tables. So many locals, so little time.

Matt and I finish drinking our hot chocolate and start to leave the diner. Just as we are about to reach the door we hear Callie call out, "Sophie, Matt! I almost forgot—are you two coming to the tree lighting ceremony tonight?"

"We wouldn't miss it!" Matt calls back. We wave as we walk to his truck and start the drive back to the cabin to relax for the rest of the day. The ceremony is tonight and I can't wait. Ever since I was a little girl, I have always felt that when those lights on the town tree turn on for the first time it means that the Christmas season is upon us. Tonight will be no different—it will feel like Christmas is finally here.

MATT

Sledding with Sophie this morning had been a blast. I honestly can't remember the last time I enjoyed myself that much. Hanging out with Sophie—even doing silly things like sledding and playing in the snow—makes my heart flutter and makes me feel like I am the luckiest man in the world. She is still the only woman who can evoke such strong emotions in me.

Now I'm sitting in my room so that Sophie can have some space to herself for the rest of the afternoon. I'm really trying to stick to this 'friends only' deal we have. Following the deal to make her happy isn't difficult, but it doesn't mean my thoughts don't stray into 'more than friends' territory. As I sit in my bedroom I imagine what it would feel like to have her back in my arms. What it would feel like to taste her lips and tangle my fingers in her long blonde hair again. I've always missed her, but I never realized how *much* until now.

All of these thoughts are going to drive me crazy if I don't find a way to distract myself. Squeezing my eyes shut and taking a deep breath, I force myself to stop thinking of Sophie. I grab my laptop and log in to my professor account for the university, hoping that work will be enough of a distraction.

A few hours later, when I have finished checking and rechecking my lesson plans for the hundredth time, I venture out of my room to see what Sophie is doing. I find her sitting on the couch in front of a fire—flames blazing in multiple colors from the pinecones she loves so much. Walking into the living room I ask, "Hey, you. What are you up to?"

"Hey. Just reading. I was beginning to think you were hiding from me for some reason," Sophie says.

"Nope. Just giving you some space. Being a good friend," I say with a smile as I sit on the other end of the couch.

"Ahhh. Makes sense now," she says with a nod. "Thanks for that."

"No problem. So, the tree lighting is in about an hour. I was thinking we should head into town soon so we can maybe look around a bit before we make our way to the tree."

"That sounds good. Let me just get ready quick and we can go." Sophie stands and makes her way down the hall to get ready while I make sure the fire is out and everything is turned off.

As we are leaving the cabin a few minutes later, the snow is gently falling and the stars are shining. "It's such a great night for the tree lighting tonight, isn't it?"

"It really is," Sophie says as she looks up at the stars and catches snowflakes on her hand. "The snow always makes the tree lighting feel more special."

I open the door and help her climb into my truck before going around to the driver's side. As we make the short drive into town we sing along to Christmas music on the radio and tease each other about being off-key. After we park, we hop out and stroll to the town square where the tree is set up.

Along the way we stop to peer in the shop windows that are beautifully decorated. Some are adorned with twinkling lights and candy canes. Others have fake snow and miniature Christmas villages. The streets are lined with vendors handing out free hot chocolate and warm cookies. Children are laughing and smiling as they wait in line to have their faces painted with various Christmas themed designs. Carolers dressed in vintage attire sing familiar holiday tunes as a crowd of people gathers around waiting for the ceremony to begin. We make our way through to an open spot up front to listen to the music, and wait for the mayor to start the night's festivities.

As we stand there, Sophie and I chat with some older women that are friends of our families. They ask us how we've been, where we are living these days, and if we are enjoying being back. Our pleasant conversation continues until, finally, the mayor comes out to stand in front of the tree and calls for everyone's attention.

"Good evening!" he shouts. "Welcome to the annual Winterglen Christmas tree lighting! I'm so happy to see so many here—both new faces and old friends. The week ahead is filled with fun, family events that everyone will love—both the young and the old. We've got the gingerbread house competition, which I know Marsha and Tom over there are anxious to defend their championship title at," he says as he points to a middle-aged couple in the middle of the crowd, "as well as a snowman building event and of course our annual ice sculpture competition and Christmas Eve dance. But first, to kick off all of the fun, we need to light this tree!" He motions behind him to the massive Christmas tree that had been decorated earlier in the week. It's covered in hundreds of glittering ornaments of different shapes and sizes, some made by the local community center art program. A giant gold star sits at the top and multi-colored lights wrap around it, waiting to be illuminated. "Help me countdown from ten and we will get this beauty lit!"

"Ten...nine...eight...," we all chant. When we get to 'one' the mayor pulls the giant red lever decorated like a candy cane and the Christmas tree sparkles with thousands of colorful lights. I steal a glance towards Sophie. Her face is lit up with a bright smile and I can see the reflection of the lights twinkling in her eyes. Seeing her so happy puts a big smile on my own face. The town tree is beautiful, but nothing will ever be as beautiful as she is to me.

Sophie turns towards me. "What?" she asks with a smile.

"Nothing. I was just—you look so happy."

"I *am* happy. This place is so *magical*. All of the decorations, the snow, being with friends," she takes my hand and gently squeezes it before letting it go, "makes me feel not as lonely without my family as I thought I would."

I smile at Sophie before we both return our gazes to the Christmas tree in front of us. Everyone around us is still cheering and clapping for the wonderful display. The mayor motions for the crowd to quiet down before leading us all in singing some Christmas carols to keep in the festive spirit. We sing favorites like *Jingle Bells* and *We Wish You A Merry Christmas,* as well as a few other tunes before the mayor ends the night with a reminder to everyone about the gingerbread house competition tomorrow afternoon. Sophie and I say our goodbyes to Callie and a few other local friends that we ran into, and start the short stroll back to my truck.

"That was so beautiful!" Sophie says as we walk. "The tree lighting was always one of my favorite events when I was growing up. It always signaled to me that Christmas was almost here."

"I always enjoyed it too," I say as we round a corner. Up ahead I see something shining on the sidewalk, but before I can warn her, Sophie slips on a patch of ice and loses her balance. I quickly stick my arm out and wrap it around her waist, catching her before she falls. As I help her stand back upright, I pull her in close to me.

She looks into my eyes nervously. "Thank you," she whispers a bit breathlessly.

"Are you alright?"

"Yeah, I'm okay. Just didn't realize it was so icy there." As much as I want to use this opportunity to kiss her, I don't want to upset her again or scare her off so I loosen my grip a little and she takes a step back. We walk the rest of the way to my truck in silence and I help her climb in.

She's quiet on the drive back to the cabin, staring out at the houses and yards decorated with bright lights and inflatable decorations. When we arrive she turns in her seat to look at me and says, "I had a really good time tonight, Matt. And again, thanks for catching me and not letting me fall."

"I had a really good time, too, Sophie."

She brushes her lips across my cheek for a quick kiss before quickly stepping out of the truck. I rush from my side to walk next to her. "Here, let me walk with you so you don't slip again," I say. We reach the door together and I open it for her, letting us both inside.

"It's pretty late so I'm going to head to bed. I'll see you in the morning," she says. I watch from the entryway as she disappears into her bedroom and closes the door.

I walk to my own room at the end of the hallway and get ready for bed. After stripping down to my boxers I crawl under the covers and fall asleep dreaming of Sophie.

When I wake up, I'm freezing. Looking over at the clock I see that it's three o'clock in the morning. I sleepily pull a blanket up from the bottom of the bed and wrap it around myself to try to get warm. As I lay here shivering, I hear a soft knock at my door. "Hey, Matt? Are you awake?"

Clearing my throat I say, "Yeah, what's wrong?"

"It's freezing in here!" Sophie shrieks. "I tried turning on some lights, but it looks like the power went out, so the heater isn't working."

I try turning on the lamp next to my bed. Sure enough the power is out. I crawl out of bed wrapped in the blanket and open the door. "Yeah, you're right. The power is out so the heater has to be out as well. Looks like you'll have to come in here with me and we can cuddle for body heat to keep us warm. For safety purposes, of course," I say with a chuckle.

"I'm not sleeping with you, Matt," she says sternly, glaring at me.

"Can't blame me for trying," I say with a wink and a shrug. "Will a fire in the fireplace be more suitable?"

"Yeah, a fire sounds great."

"Okay, just give me one second," I say as I turn back towards my bed. I find a flashlight in the drawer of the table next to my bed, join Sophie who is holding her own flashlight, and we wander out to the living room together—both wrapped in blankets—to start the fire. I gather some wood from the bin next to the fireplace while Sophie finds some matches in the kitchen. A few minutes later I have the fire started and we sit down on the couch together to wait for the chill to fade. We sit in silence, both still half asleep from the early hour, and listen to the wood crackle in the fireplace.

I'm the first to break the silence when I say, "You can sleep on the couch. I'll take the floor."

"Are you sure? I don't mind sleeping on the floor."

"Absolutely not. I'm not letting you sleep on the floor. I'd rather freeze in my room before I ever let you sleep on the floor."

Sophie smiles at me. "You're still as sweet as ever."

"I try."

"Well thank you then. For giving me the couch, I mean." She hands me a pillow.

"You sure you don't want to cuddle to stay warm?"

"Goodnight, Matt," she says, rolling her eyes.

"Goodnight, Sophie," I sigh taking the pillow and my blanket to make a place to sleep on the floor in front of the fireplace. I would have preferred sleeping with Sophie in my bed, wrapped in my arms, pushed up against me, but at least I am sleeping close to her tonight. She's close enough that I can smell the fresh strawberry scent of her shampoo. I gaze over at her on the couch—her eyes closed—and smile to myself as I drift off to sleep at the way the fire glows softly against her cheeks.

SOPHIE

When I wake up, it takes me a minute to figure out where I am. I feel a little stiff and like something has been pushing into my back all night. I blink my eyes a few times until the room comes into focus. I am in the living room on the couch, the fireplace is still smoldering from a fire that has recently burned out, and Matt is sleeping on the floor—on his stomach with one arm tucked under his pillow, blankets kicked to the side, wearing nothing but a pair of boxers.

I remember that we came to the living room to stay warm after the power had gone out last night, but I hadn't seen what he was wearing. It had been too dark and he was wrapped in a large blanket. Seeing him lying here now, sound asleep, I can't help but take my time to admire him. His back rippling with muscles—more muscles than he had had back when we were younger. He always had big muscles due to his football playing days in high school, but now that he is older he has filled out nicely. His boxers hug his tight, defined ass and I want to run my hands over it, but I can't. Touching him would be a mistake. I'm pretty sure that would break the friendship barrier.

Kissing him last night, even though it had only been a kiss on his cheek, had reignited my desire to be with him. When he had invited me into his bed last night, it had taken all of my willpower to say no. Matt has been doing his best to earn my trust back, but so far I'm still not ready to take it to the next step. After what he did to me after high school it will take a lot more than two days to earn my trust back.

At that moment Matt begins to stir. I look away quickly so that he won't catch me daydreaming about him. "Morning, sleepyhead," I say.

"Morning, Sophie." He looks at me with his big sleepy blue eyes. His eyes have always reminded me of the ocean. They are the prettiest shade of blue that I have ever seen.

"I was thinking of signing up for the gingerbread house competition today. Want to be my partner?"

"Sure. My mom and I used to enter that competition every year, if you remember. I'd love to do it again."

"Well I'm not sure if my gingerbread house building skills will be up to par with your mom's, but I'll try my best. The last time I made one was probably the last time my family and I were here for Christmas."

"No worries. I haven't made one since high school either," he says with a laugh.

"Okay then, let's go sign up after breakfast." I stand up from my spot on the couch and head for my room to deposit the blanket I had used last night while Matt makes sure that the fire is completely out.

We meet in the kitchen after we are both showered and dressed. "Anything specific you want for breakfast?" Matt asks.

"Something quick is fine for me this morning," I say. "Is there anything specific that *you* want?"

"No, I'm good with cereal and toast. Does that work for you?"

"That's prefect—quick and simple." I head over to the counter to grab the bread and put it in the toaster while Matt pours cereal into bowls. When the toast is finished we carry our food over to the table and sit down to eat.

"Did you sleep well last night?" he asks.

"I slept alright. I was a little stiff this morning from sleeping on the couch, but it wasn't too bad. How about you?"

"I slept fine. I can pretty much fall asleep anywhere so the floor didn't bother me at all."

"That's good at least," I say with a smile as I take another bite of my cereal.

We finish up breakfast, chatting about the day ahead, and then get ready to go. Matt and I drive into town and head to city hall, where the competition is being held, to sign up. We take the stairs down to the auditorium level—following the snowflakes and gingerbread men signs— and find that the room is already filled with people. As we walk in I hear a high-pitched squeal seconds before arms are flung around my neck and I am enveloped in a hug by Trisha, my best friend from high school.

"Oh my god! Why didn't you tell me that you were coming into town for the holidays?" Trisha asks excitedly.

I laugh. "Hey, Trisha. I didn't tell anybody I was coming into town because I wanted it to be a surprise. I had hoped to see you at the tree lighting last night, but I didn't see you there."

"Yeah, I was really bummed about not being there, but I got called into work. Life of an emergency room nurse," she shrugs.

Finally noticing who I was standing with, Trisha looks between Matt and I. She gasps and covers her mouth with her hand. "Are you two back together?" she squeals.

"No, but we are friends again. Turns out we both rented the same cabin for Christmas vacation, so we decided to make the best of it."

Matt nods. "Hi, Trisha."

"Hi, Matt. Don't break my best friend's heart this time," she says pointedly, shoving a finger into his chest. "Otherwise I will track you down and hurt you this time."

"I would never hurt her again," Matt says sheepishly as he hangs his head.

"It's okay," I say grabbing Matt's hand and giving it a reassuring squeeze. "It's Christmas and we're not going to dwell on the past anymore." I drop his hand quickly, feeling the familiar butterflies in my stomach from the contact of his skin against mine.

Turning back to Trisha I ask, "Are you competing in the gingerbread house competition?"

"Not this year—I'm judging this time."

"Awesome! Where do Matt and I go to sign up?"

"Over there to that long table," she says pointing to the table at the other end of the room.

"Thanks. We'll see you later!" I say as Matt and I make our way to the sign-up table. Callie and Mr. Elliott are sitting behind the table signing in competitors. I see that Marsha and Tom—the defending champions—have already signed in, as well as a few of the other teams.

"Good morning, you two!" Mr. Elliott says cheerfully. "Are you here to watch or to sign up?"

"Here to sign up, of course," I say with a bright smile.

"In that case, here you go," says Callie handing a clipboard to Matt with the sign-up sheet.

"Thanks," Matt says as he starts to write the required information.

After filling out our names and finding our worktable, Matt and I set to work coming up with a plan for our design. We will have one hour to build the most creative gingerbread house once the competition starts. All of the supplies that we will need are provided for us. There are cookie cutters, knives, spatula spreaders, frosting, candies, and of course gingerbread.

We brainstorm ideas for a few minutes before finally agreeing on a design that will look like a miniature version of our town. It will be a big undertaking, one that will be risky to pull off in an hour—especially since neither of us has done this in ten years—but Matt and I love a good competition and we are willing to take the big risk.

The announcer—who is the city clerk—gets everyone's attention, sets the timer to one hour, and rings the bell to start the competition. Matt and I get to work right away. We work together to cut the pieces of gingerbread into the shapes for the main buildings that we want to showcase. We are making Mr. Elliott's hardware store, Callie's Diner, the post office, and the toy store. Matt works on cutting the walls while I work on cutting the pieces for the roofs. When we are finished cutting out the shapes we start working on pasting them together with the frosting—Matt holding the pieces together while I gently line the edges with the glue-like frosting. Once that is all done we both start working on decorating.

Our entry has a row of shops that line main street with the town square in the middle and the big Christmas tree in the center. We don't have enough time to add in any of the little houses that we had planned on adding, but the main focus that we want to have is on the shops anyway.

"Alright folks, we have about ten seconds left!" shouts the announcer. "Ten…nine…eight…" I can hear the crowd counting down excitedly. "…three…two…one!" We have just finished putting the final touches on when the announcer calls out that time is up. Matt and I look at each other and smile, giving each other a high five.

"Nice work, Sophie," Matt says.

"You too! I think we did a really great job."

"Mission accomplished. Now we just have to wait for the judging."

The judges take their time walking around the room, taking in all of the wonderful creations that have been made. The people in the crowd are all chatting excitedly, while those of us who are contestants are all standing around nervously. When they reach our table, they smile as they make notes on their clipboards. A few of them, including Trisha nod, as one of the other judges whispers something.

While the judges deliberate, Matt and I talk with some of the other contestants. Marsha and Tom are at the table next to ours and we tell them that their creation is incredible—they have made an entire Santa's village. Another couple nearby comment about what a cool idea we had to make the town of Winterglen. As the judges take their positions at the front of the room we all head back to our tables. When it is time for the winners to be announced, Matt nudges me and whispers, "We've got this." I smile back at him and wait for the announcement.

Trisha steps up to the microphone up front, "Hello everyone! I had the pleasure of judging all of your beautiful creations this year, along with my fellow judges, and let me just say that it was not an easy decision. So many wonderful gingerbread houses to choose from." There is a round of applause. "After much deliberation, we have decided that this year's winners of the Winterglen gingerbread competition are…….Sophie Lebeau and Matt O'Connor!"

"Yes!" I squeal while Matt pumps his fist in the air. He turns and picks me up, wrapping me in a hug and spinning me around as I laugh.

"Told you we had it," he says with a chuckle.

I suddenly realize that he is still holding me in his arms. We're too close. I feel hot and his closeness is doing things to me that it shouldn't. "Put me down, Matt," I say sternly.

"Huh? Oh, sorry," he says shyly as he lowers me

to the ground, swallowing hard. "I—uh—got carried away."

"It's alright," I say as I straighten my clothes and try to catch my own breath before he sees that he has effected me.

"Come on up here, you two!" says Trisha.

We walk up to the front of the room to shake hands with all of the judges. Trisha presents us with a trophy in the shape of a gingerbread man. "Congratulations on first place!" She gives each of us a hug and says, "I knew you could do it!"

After being congratulated by Marsha and Tom, Callie, Mr. Elliott, and several spectators, we gather our belongings, plus our winning creation and our shiny trophy. I help Matt carry the large board holding our gingerbread town as we climb the stairs up to the main level. Thankfully, the doors have been propped open so that contestants can easily exit the building with their showpieces.

"We still make a good team," Matt says as we walk to his truck.

"Yeah, I guess we do." I think for a moment before adding sadly, "For some things anyway."

He stays silent for a minute before he stops walking and answers. "We make a good team for everything, Sophie. I was just an idiot and ruined that. But I'm smarter now—I *know* that I made a mistake. Will you ever give me a second chance to make it right?"

I search his eyes. I can see the sincerity in them and I can tell that he is hurting over what he had done in the past. "Maybe someday, Matt. I'm not ready yet, though."

"That's fair enough," he says sadly before we start walking again.

It's true. Maybe someday I can give him a second chance, but I don't want things between us to move too fast. I want more time as friends to ease myself back into a relationship with him. The last thing I want is to let him back in too quickly and have a repeat of the last time he ended things.

MATT

After the gingerbread competition Sophie and I drive to the local steakhouse to grab a celebration dinner. I want to talk a little bit more about what is happening between us. I also want to tell her that I understand her reluctance to get back together with me, but that I will do everything in my power to show her that she can trust me with her heart again.

Once we arrive at the steakhouse and have ordered steaks and wine, I glance across at Sophie nervously. "So, I know you just told me that you aren't ready to give me a second chance—and that's fine, I get it—but I need you to know that I will do anything to prove to you that you can trust me again. I want us to be able to enjoy being with each other, like we used to."

"I want that too, Matt. And like I said, I'm not ready yet, but I hope that some day I will be," Sophie says.

"I know you've probably hated me for what I did, but I hope that eventually you can forgive me."

"I've never *hated* you, Matt. I just didn't particularly like you very much for a while," Sophie chuckles as she takes a sip of her wine. "But I have forgiven you. That's why we're working on this friendship thing, remember?"

Smiling at her I say, "Thank you for telling me. I feel better knowing that I'm forgiven."

Sophie gives me a serious look before she says softly, "Don't make me regret it, Matt."

"I won't. I promise."

We finish the rest of our dinner, including a chocolate lava cake that we share for dessert, and make our way back to the cabin. When we arrive, we make the usual fire in the fireplace and turn the Christmas tree lights on. The soft glow from the fire and the twinkling of the tree lights is perfect as we sit together on the couch looking through photos that Sophie's sister Jessica emailed to her earlier.

"I'm so jealous that she gets to spend Christmas in Paris," Sophie says. "I've always thought that it would be an amazing experience."

"Looking at these pictures, it looks like it *is* an amazing experience."

"I'm really glad Jessica is having such a great time. I know that Christmas has always been a time that we've spent with our family and this year is just so different. I was worried that she would be homesick. It's nice to see that she's not."

"How are *you* doing—not being with your family this year?" I ask.

"I'm alright. I mean, I miss my family—but spending time with you hasn't been *so* bad," she says with a shy smile. "And being back here in Winterglen makes it more bearable."

"Well, I'm here for you if you need me." A piece of hair falls loose from her ponytail and I tuck it back behind her ear. I feel so comfortable around Sophie and the simple movement comes instinctually. I can feel her body tense and hear her sharp intake of breath. "I'll always be here if you need me." I look into her eyes.

She turns away and nods, "I know." She clears her throat and moves to go into the kitchen. "I need something to drink. Would you like anything?"

"Sure. I'll have whatever you're having."

She comes back carrying two glasses of eggnog and hands me one. Taking a sip, I can taste that she added some rum. "I thought you didn't like rum."

"Maybe my tastes have changed."

"Have they?" I ask skeptically.

"No, but rum is all I could find," she says sticking her tongue out at me.

I laugh. "Have I really driven you to drink, Sophie? You're so bothered by my touch that you're willing to drink alcohol in any form?"

"I'm not bothered by your touch," she replies defiantly. "I just needed a drink, that's all. Maybe looking at those pictures from my sister affected me more than I thought."

I'm not sure that I completely believe her on that, but I'm not going to push her. I don't want to say something that will push her away again. I feel like we're finally in a good place. Like she said earlier tonight, she's not ready to trust me in a relationship yet, but I will take whatever I can get at this point. As long as she is in my life, I'm happy.

Finishing my eggnog, I stand up and tell Sophie that I need to take a shower before bed. We made plans to go into town tomorrow for the day to browse the main street shops and to see what other fun we can find. Tomorrow night is the sleigh rides and ice skating at the outdoor rink that the town sets up near the town square. Those two events had always been some of mine and Sophie's favorites to attend when we were teenagers, so I'm looking forward to recreating the memories again. I'm hoping that it will bring back some happy memories for Sophie, too, and maybe create some new ones.

After gathering my toothbrush, toothpaste, and a clean pair of boxers from my room I head back to the bathroom to take a shower. I walk into the bathroom and set my things down on the counter before closing the door behind me. Reaching in, I turn the water on to let it warm up and then get undressed.

Before I can get into the shower my cell phone buzzes. I pick it up and glance at the screen. It's a text message from Dean Sanders, the dean of the university and my boss. As I open the message I curse to myself. It's not a message from Dean Sanders—it's from his daughter, my crazy stalker Victoria. She has been calling and texting me almost daily since we met over a year ago, and I thought I had successfully blocked her number, but she always manages to find a way to contact me. I can't exactly block the number of my boss—I'm just surprised it took Victoria this long to realize that she could reach me by using his phone.

I quickly read the message.

Matt—it's Victoria. Where ARE you? I stopped by your apartment, but you weren't there and your landlord said he hasn't seen you in a few days. Why have you been avoiding me? I want to see you.

I hit the delete message button without responding before turning my phone off completely and tossing it onto the bathroom counter. For now, keeping my phone off is the best way to avoid Victoria. Later I can think of a way to avoid her without blocking Dean Sanders' number.

Stepping into the shower, I stand under the hot spray of water and let it relax me. Being with Sophie for the last few days had almost made me forget about my problems with my stalker, but now Victoria is crashing back into my life when I least want her to. Winning Sophie back will be hard enough—adding Victoria into the mix will make it even more difficult. I need to think of a way to make sure that Sophie never has to encounter her. I don't want to hide anything from Sophie, especially since

I'm trying to regain her trust, but I really don't want her to have to deal with all of the drama that Victoria brings to my life. Maybe it's best if I just keep the text message to myself and don't say anything to Sophie.

As I wash up and finish showering, I let my mind drift back to thoughts of tomorrow night's events. Ice skating is happening first, which will be a good way to have some fun together and then we can relax and talk on the sleigh ride. I haven't been ice skating in years, so at the very least Sophie will get a good laugh out of it. Hopefully I don't fall too many times. Who knows—maybe Sophie hasn't skated in a while either and we will be holding each other up.

After I've dried off, brushed my teeth, and slipped on my clean boxers, I grab my cell phone and start heading back to my room. As I pass by Sophie's door I hear the faint sound of *Jingle Bells* coming from inside her room. "Oh what fun it is to ride in a one horse open sleigh-eh!" I hear her singing along to Christmas music and I can't help but chuckle and smile to myself. Christmas music has always been a favorite part of the holiday for me and hearing her sing along to some of my favorite songs makes me elated. I hum along to the tune as I make it back to my room. I crawl into bed and lay awake for a while, thinking about Sophie and all of the happy times we used to have. Holding her in my arms would be the perfect ending to this night, but thoughts of her will have to do for now. I fall into a deep sleep, dreaming of Sophie.

SOPHIE

*L*ast night after Matt had excused himself to go take a shower, I had gone into my bedroom and turned on some Christmas music. Singing along to my favorite songs was the only thing I could think of to distract myself from my feelings and my thoughts about Matt naked in the shower with water rippling down his toned muscles.

It worked for a little while, but then I heard Matt walking past my bedroom and I couldn't help but let my mind wander to thoughts of him. It had been a restless night of sleep after that and now it is becoming abundantly clear that I can't avoid my feelings for him much longer. Do I just give in to my emotions or should I stay on this path that my brain is telling me to follow?

This morning when I woke up—after the few hours I actually managed to sleep— the sun was shining through my curtains and I had peeked outside to see the snow sparkling like diamonds. The trees are covered with the shimmery white powder and the yard is blanketed with a few new inches of snow. This view is why I am now standing outside, sipping a cup of hot chocolate, and enjoying every minute of it. Well, almost every minute, in between contemplating my feelings for Matt.

I told Matt yesterday that I'm not ready to try a relationship with him again, but I honestly don't know if I can remain just friends. My heart and my mind don't seem to be on the same page with that. My head is telling me to stay friends and not to trust him, but my heart is screaming at me to take him back and never let him go. Tonight we are supposed to go ice skating and on a sleigh ride and I'm not sure if I can refrain from acting on my feelings. Those two events were always special to us as teenagers and I have a feeling my heart is about to win the argument with my head.

As I look out on the snowy scene in front of me, I hear the door to the cabin open and Matt step outside. "Good morning," I say as he comes up beside me.

"Morning, Sophie. What are you doing out here on this beautiful morning?"

"Just enjoying the view. It snowed last night and the sun shining on the snow made it glisten. I just couldn't resist coming outside and taking this all in."

"Yeah—there's just something special about a fresh snowfall that makes this town even more beautiful," he says.

"Are you ready for tonight? When is the last time you went ice skating?" I ask teasingly.

"It's been a few years and I might be a little rusty," he laughs.

"That's alright. I won't make fun of you *too* much." I nudge his shoulder playfully.

He smiles at that. "We should probably get ready to go into town to look at the shops."

"Sounds good to me. Let's stop at the diner for breakfast first."

"Sounds good."

Going back inside we get ready to go and then make our way to Callie's Diner. When we arrive we find a booth near the back and sit down. A few minutes later a waitress comes over to take our order.

"Hi!" says the bubbly young waitress. "What can I get for you two this morning?"

"I'll take the Christmas pancakes with a side of bacon and a hot chocolate please," I say. The Christmas pancakes are a special treat this time of year at Callie's. They are pancakes topped with a white chocolate peppermint syrup. Absolutely the most heavenly dish ever created.

"That sounds great! I'll have the same, please," says Matt.

"Great choices!" says our waitress. "Coming right up!" she says as she turns and walks away to put our order in.

As we wait for our food Matt and I discuss our plans for the rest of the day. "So, what should we do after breakfast? Ice skating isn't until later, so we have some time to do something else," I say.

"I thought we were planning to go look around the shops? I wouldn't mind doing some Christmas shopping for my family. The shops here always have some unique gifts that I wouldn't be able to find in the city."

"Well, I didn't plan on doing much shopping since I want to save it for the village market later, but it never hurts to look, I guess. There might be some different options than the market, and you're right—I might find something that I wouldn't be able to find in Chicago." Our food arrives a short while later and we immediately dig in. "Mmmm—this is as delicious as I remember," I say.

"I haven't had Callie's Christmas pancakes in years. These really are the best," Matt says as he takes another bite.

We continue to eat the rest of our breakfast while we keep discussing our plans. After we are done and pay our bill we make our way down the street to the shops. I plan on doing most of my shopping at the Christmas village market later this week, but maybe I can find a few things at the shops today too.

Matt and I wander from shop to shop for the next hour, browsing through all of the collections. "Oooh—look at this, Matt!" I say as I hold up a beautifully hand-crafted wooden 'Winterglen Is Home Sweet Home' sign. "My parents would *love* this. So much of our life was spent here."

Matt smiles. "I think you're right. They'll love it. I think your mom would also love this," he says as he shows me the locally made wine. "I remember she used to always have a bottle of this at the holidays."

"You're right," I say as I take the bottle from him. "I think your mom is going to love the locally hand-crafted ornaments you found, too! They'll look beautiful in her collection. The Winterglen hat and coffee mug will be great for your dad. He was always happy with a new shirt or hat." I smile at the memory.

"He still is," Matt says with a laugh.

We both find a few more small items for our families and then head back to the cabin. We still have a few hours until ice skating starts so we have time to relax for a bit. I use the time to do a little reading, while Matt showers and changes clothes.

At five o'clock we drive back into town and go over to the outdoor rink that has been set up near City Hall. We both rent a pair of skates from the booth that has been set up for the few people that don't have ice skates or forgot them. Sitting on the bench, I quickly lace up my skates and jump up. "Ready to go, Matt?"

He chuckles as he finishes lacing up his own skates. "As ready as I'll ever be I guess."

We walk over to the edge and I step onto the ice first. I love ice skating—I took all of the lessons when I was a kid—and I still skate as often as I can. Matt slowly steps onto the ice behind me, holding on to the little wall that is around the edge of the rink. He hesitantly tries to glide while holding onto the wall as I skate backwards in front of him. I cover my mouth with my hand, trying to hide my smile, but I'm unable to stop the giggle that escapes as he nearly stumbles forward.

"Don't laugh," he chuckles. "I told you it's been a long time since I was on skates last."

"Oh come on. It's like riding a bike! Once you learn, you never forget!"

"True. I haven't forgotten *how*—but that doesn't mean I'm not a little rusty on the whole balancing on a small blade on the ice part though," he says.

I smile at him and grab his hands, pulling him away from the wall. "Just hold on to me then."

We skate around the rink, Matt regaining his confidence as we go. I wave as I see Trisha skating with her family and say hello to a few other people as we pass by. As we skate, a song comes on over the speakers. Not just any song—*THE* song. The one that Matt and I used to dance to at *all* of our high school dances. *Our* song.

Turning to me he says, "Come on. Let's dance for old time's sake."

"We're on skates," I laugh.

"So? We *skate* dance then." He grabs my waist and pulls me close as he spins us around in small circles. I feel his warm breath on the side of my cold face, his body pressing as close to mine as our winter jackets will allow. Suddenly, I no longer feel cold—my body is heating up from his closeness. Everything around me seems to fade away, and it's as if we are the only two people on the ice, moving to the slow rhythm of the music as we look into each other's eyes.

As the song ends, he reluctantly pulls away and we start skating around the rink again. I'm no longer focused on skating though as my mind is reeling with thoughts of how badly I want Matt. I somehow manage to make it through the rest of skating and when it's all over we head back to the benches to take our skates off.

"That was exhilarating!" Matt says happily.

"It was a lot of fun! Reminded me of a lot of great memories, too," I say as I check the time. "Let's go over to take our sleigh ride."

We walk over to stand in line for the sleigh rides. A lot of people have already made their way over from the ice rink, but there aren't too many in front of us. When it is finally our turn, Matt helps me into the sleigh and climbs in behind me. He sits down and covers our laps with the blanket that is provided and soon we are on our way.

It's a beautiful night—the stars are twinkling up above and a light snow is gently falling. Christmas lights are wrapped around the trees throughout the town, and are shimmering softly along the route. The street has been blocked off for the sleigh rides, so the only sound is the soft clip-clop of the horses hooves plodding along against the snow-covered road. As the horse-drawn sleigh slowly pulls us through town, I shiver.

"Are you cold?" Matt asks as he puts his arm around me.

I snuggle into him, breathing in his sandalwood scent. "A little." I stare up into his eyes and see the slightest bit of shock there before he tightens his arm around me. I've been arguing with myself all day about whether or not I should act on my feelings. My heart finally wins out and I lean up to gently brush my lips against his. I hear his startled gasp at first, but soon enough he is kissing me back. He parts my lips with his tongue and deepens our kiss. His fingers thread through my hair as he cradles the back of my head. When we finally come up for air we are both a bit breathless.

"Wow. What was that for?" he asks.

"I can't fight it anymore. I want you, Matt. I always have."

He searches my face. "You want to give us another chance?"

"I do. I feel like I can trust you again." He kisses me again and we cuddle together as the sleigh continues to pull us through the town. I lean my head on his shoulder and he wraps his arm tightly around me, pulling me into him, as the sleigh slowly makes its way back to where we started.

When we get to the end of our ride Matt wraps his arms around my waist and lifts me out of the sleigh before we quickly walk back to his truck, hand in hand. The tension has been building between us all week and now that we've kissed it's reached its peak. We need to get home and we need to get there *now*.

MATT

We're both silent as I drive to the cabin as quickly as the snowy road allows. I keep one hand on the steering wheel and the other hand on Sophie's thigh throughout the drive. I can tell that she wants this just as badly as I do. We arrive at the cabin and both jump out of the truck and rush to the front door.

Sophie laughs as she reaches for my hand and says, "Hurry up, Matt! Let's go!"

"Are you in a hurry to get somewhere?" I tease as she pulls me to the door.

"Yes! Now, come on!"

Sophie unlocks the door and pushes it open, flipping on a light as we step inside. I pull her in for another kiss that I've been yearning for since the last one on the sleigh while stripping her out of her jacket. She holds on to my jacket collar as I lead her into the living room, kissing her the entire way. Ever since that night we slept out here together I've been dreaming of getting her naked and making love to her in front of the fireplace.

"What are we doing, Matt? I thought we were going to the bedroom."

"We'll get there eventually. But first—I've been dreaming of this for days," I say with a smile as I flip the switch for the fireplace to roar to life. Sophie pushes off my jacket and pulls me into her arms, wrapping them around my neck as she crushes her mouth against mine.

Grabbing a blanket off of the couch, I lay her down on top of it and settle myself on top of her, supporting my weight with my forearms.

"You've dreamt of having sex with me on the living room floor?" Sophie asks teasingly, raising an eyebrow.

"Yes—in front of this cozy fire and our Christmas tree," I say as I plant kisses starting at her mouth and trailing down the side of her neck.

"I've thought about it a few times too."

Bringing my mouth down onto hers, I kiss her passionately while running my hands down the sides of her body and then back up to cup her breasts through the fabric of her sweater. As I rub her nipples through the fabric, Sophie moans and digs her fingernails into my back.

She breaks our kiss long enough to say, "Please, Matt. I need to feel your hands on me."

Sitting up just enough, I reach for the hem of her shirt and pull it up over her head. I take my time tracing my fingers along her waist before finally unclasping her bra. Seeing her beautiful bare breasts makes my cock even harder than it already was. As I'm admiring the sight in front of me, she rocks her hips up into me. Even through our jeans the contact is almost enough to make me cum—but I'll be damned if I'm going to cum before I have the time to thoroughly enjoy being inside of her. "Damn, woman! You're going to make me cum just looking at you if you keep that up!" I chuckle.

Sophie giggles and pulls me closer. "Then quit teasing and let's make up for lost time."

I unfasten my belt and push my jeans and boxers down to my ankles then kick them off. Sophie moves to take off her own pants, but I say "Uh-uh. I've been wanting to take your pants off since the first day I saw you standing in front of me in this cabin. Allow me." I slowly slide her jeans down and she is left wearing only her white lacy panties.

Moving between her legs, I kiss along her inner thigh and then kiss down the center of the lacy fabric. I can feel Sophie shuddering as I pull the lacy fabric to the side and slip my tongue up and down along her slit.

"Please, Matt," she groans as she tugs at my hair.

I slide her panties off and then continue to suck and lick at her clit until she is writhing beneath my tongue. Her pussy tastes amazing and she's dripping wet, melting beneath my mouth. She screams out my name as she orgasms with the next flick of my tongue. I keep licking and hold onto her tight ass as another orgasm rips through her.

"Uhh—that feels so good—I need you inside me—," Sophie pants.

Pulling back I wipe my face with my hand and reach for my discarded jeans to pull a condom out of my pocket. Ripping it open, I roll it on over my cock —which is hard as a rock now—and line my dick up with her entrance. She looks up at me in anticipation while biting her lip. I surge inside her in one smooth motion and we both moan in pleasure.

"Fuck, you feel so good Sophie." She wraps her

legs around my waist as I pump into her, again and again.

Without separating, I roll us over so that she is on top of me now, riding my cock. I thrust my hips up as her eyes close and her head falls back, her beautiful blonde hair cascading in waves behind her.

Using my thumb I reach between us and rub her clit. "Oh, fuck," she says at the extra stimulation. "I'm going to cum, Matt." I feel her clench tightly around my dick as her orgasm takes her over the edge. A few more quick, hard thrusts and I grunt as my own release comes.

She gently falls on top of me, resting her head on my chest. I rub her back as we both lie here panting and sweaty, tangled in the blanket. When I finally go soft inside her, she rolls off. I pull out, remove the condom, and throw it in the trash.

Lying in front of the cozy fire, with Sophie snuggled in my arms, everything feels right in my life again. I gently kiss the top of her head as I press her closer into the side of my body.

She looks up at me with a smile on her face as she rubs her fingers along my chest. "I've missed you, Matt."

"I've missed you too, Sophie," I say as I kiss her

beautiful mouth. "Thank you—for giving me another chance."

"I want to make us work this time, Matt. No matter what—I need you in my life."

"I need *you* in my life, too, Sophie." From now on, I plan to do everything to show her just how *much* I need her in my life.

We make love in front of the fire a few more times before finally drifting off to sleep in each other's arms.

SOPHIE

The familiar sound of my cell phone ringing breaks me out of my deep sleep. From the specific ringtone I can tell that it's Trisha calling so I decide to let it go to voicemail and call her back later—I'm so comfortable that I'm not ready to move just yet.

Matt's arm is wrapped around my waist and I can smell his familiar scent. I smile to myself as I snuggle in closer to him. Last night was incredible and I plan on repeating it as much as possible.

"Morning," Matt says sleepily. "How did you sleep?"

"Morning," I say grinning up at him. "I haven't slept that well in forever."

"Me neither," he says. "Was that your phone ringing?"

"Yeah—just Trisha. I will call her back in a little while," I mumble as I nuzzle into the side of his neck.

"Mmm." He groans as I nip at him with my teeth and slide my hand down his chiseled abs to his cock. I hear his sharp intake of breath as my hand wraps around his hard length, stroking up and down.

Kissing my way down his body, I can hear his breathing becoming quicker. I flick my tongue out and lick right under the head of his cock.

"Fuck!" Matt hisses.

I smile as I wrap my mouth around him, and continue to lick and suck all down his dick. His hands tangle into my hair as he moves my head and thrusts into my mouth again and again.

"Sophie, I want to be inside of you," he says.

As I nod, he pulls out of my mouth and reaches for a condom and rolls it on. Crawling on top of him I line his cock up with my entrance and I slowly push down as we both moan with pleasure.

I roll my hips as he guides me up and down. We move together, slow at first and then faster. Matt cups my ass in his hands as his mouth finds my nipple and he sucks it into his mouth. I cry out his name as I pant for breath. The sensation of his tongue rolling around my nipple as he continues to thrust into me is driving me wild. A few more thrusts and we are both crying out in ecstasy before collapsing back down onto the blanket, breathing hard.

"I think I like this whole making up for lost time thing," Matt says as he tries to catch his breath.

"Me too," I giggle.

Once we have both recovered from our morning love making session and gotten showered and dressed I pick up my phone and call Trisha back.

"Hey!" she says when she answers. "I tried calling you this morning, but you must have still been sleeping."

"Ummm—yeah, I was….sleeping. What's up?"

"I was just wondering if you wanted to grab a cup of hot chocolate with me this afternoon and catch up. We haven't really had a chance to talk much since you've been back in town."

"Sure! That would be great. How about I meet you in a half hour at the diner?"

"Sounds good. I will see you there!" Trisha says before hanging up.

When I hang up the phone I wander into the living room to find Matt. "Trisha invited me into town to hang out for a while. I'm going to go meet up with her and then I'll be back later."

"Sounds good. I was thinking since there isn't much going on tonight maybe we can order a pizza and watch Christmas movies," Matt says questioningly.

"Yeah, that sounds good to me."

"Okay good. I'll see you later then. Have fun and tell Trisha I said hi."

"Okay, I will." I slip on my jacket and boots. "See you later, Matt," I say as I walk out the door and head to my car.

When I walk into Callie's Diner a little while later I look around and find Trisha waving to me from a booth in the back.

"Good morning, Sophie" she says as I sit down across from her.

"Good morning."

"I ordered us some hot chocolate. So—how's everything going with sharing the cabin?"

"It's going good," I reply sleepily.

The waitress comes over and sets our hot chocolates down. "Just good?" asks Trisha as she takes a sip. "Is that why you're blushing?"

"Well—Matt and I—we sort of had sex last night."

Trisha almost chokes on her hot chocolate and

her eyes go wide. "You *sort of* had sex last night? Or you *did* have sex last night?"

"We *did*. Multiple times—and maybe once again this morning."

Trisha snorts and chuckles. "I knew you hadn't been sleeping when I called this morning."

"Well—we had so much fun ice skating yesterday and then on the sleigh ride, I just couldn't help it and I kissed him. Which led to me saying that I wanted to give him another chance—which then led to the sex."

"I knew when I saw you two together the other day that it was bound to happen sooner or later." Trisha's expression turns serious. "Just be careful okay, Sophie? I don't want to see my best friend's heart broken again."

"Don't worry. I'll be careful."

Trisha and I finish our drinks and decide to walk around the little Christmas village for a while to continue catching up. Even though we are best friends we haven't had much time to talk over the last few years since we both have such busy lives. We spend the rest of the morning—and part of the afternoon—just chatting about work, family, and life.

"So how are your mom and dad doing? And what about Jessica?" Trisha asks as we stroll along.

"They're all doing great! My parents were really excited for their trip this year, and Jessica is having a good time in Paris."

"Oh, that's right! I forgot you said she was going to Paris when we talked last. That has to be fun."

"Yeah, she says it is. How about your family? How are all of your brothers and sisters?" I ask. We used to all spend a lot of time together when we were growing up. I've always considered Trisha to be like another sister to me, and her parents and siblings are like a second family to me.

"They're all doing great. Actually, they are all going to be here for Christmas—staying at my house," Trisha says with a slight grimace.

I laugh. "Oh, it won't be *that* bad! You love your family!"

"True, but my house is going to be overrun by people," she says with a grin. "Seriously though, it will be nice. All of my nieces and nephews—I don't get to see them enough. Work keeps me too busy. Enough about that—any exciting plans for tonight?" Trisha asks.

"Not really exciting—but Matt and I are going to order pizza and watch our favorite Christmas movies. What about you?"

"I've got to work tonight. Hopefully it's not too

exciting, but then again, working in the ER usually is."

"Well, I will cross my fingers for you that nothing too exciting happens," I say.

"Thanks," Trisha says. "Well—I've had a great afternoon catching up with you, but I should get going so I can run home and change into my scrubs. I need to get to the hospital a little before my shift starts tonight to take care of some things."

"Alright. I had a great time too. I'll see you again before Christmas I'm sure."

"Definitely. Have a fun—*movie*—night," she says with a smirk.

"Oh shut up," I say with a laugh.

I wave as Trisha leaves and I make my way to my car. Spending the day with my best friend was nice, but now I'm looking forward to my night with Matt.

MATT

Sophie has been gone all day and I'm looking forward to her coming back to the cabin. I've had a relaxing day of reading, mostly —and I'm glad that she is spending time catching up with Trisha—but I can't wait to have her back in my arms again.

I get to work setting up our favorite Christmas movie and order pizza so that it's all ready when she gets here. I clean off the small coffee table in the center of the room for dinner before reaching into the wood bin and grabbing a couple of logs to light a wood fire in the fireplace since I know that she prefers wood instead of gas. I can't say I blame her— the smell from the burning logs and the popping sound from the flames makes the atmosphere feel so much more festive.

I'm just about to grab some extra blankets for the couch when my phone rings. Looking at the caller ID on my screen I see that it's the hospital in Chicago. My heart starts to race as a million thoughts run through my head. What happened? My parents and grandparents all live there—what if something has happened to one of them? My hands shaking, I answer my phone. "Hello?"

"Hey, baby. I've been trying to reach you and you haven't been answering my calls or texts. I miss you."

My hand tightens around my phone and the panic is replaced with anger as I recognize the voice. "What the hell, Victoria? Why are you calling me from the hospital?"

"I came to visit a sick friend and I just needed to hear your voice," she says sweetly.

"Well stop calling me Victoria. I told you to leave me alone."

"Come on, Matt. You don't really mean that. And it's Christmas—I want to spend it with you. Where are you?"

"I'm not spending it with you and it's none of your business where I am!" I shout as I hang up the phone.

At that moment Sophie walks in the door. "Is everything alright, Matt?" she asks as she places her keys on the counter. "I heard you shouting."

I take a deep breath to calm myself down before answering. "Everything's fine. It was just an unwanted phone call."

"Are you sure? You seem really upset."

"I'm fine. It's nothing. Don't worry about it, okay?" I say as I wrap my arms around her waist and lean down to kiss her lips. The second we touch it feels like all of my anger evaporates and I'm relaxed again. I love how she has this effect on me.

Sophie smiles up at me. "Are you ready for movie night?" I ask her.

"Definitely. I've been looking forward to it all day—and I'm starving."

The doorbell rings. "Well, lucky for you—that's the pizza." I grab my wallet and open the door to pay the delivery driver for the food.

After locking the door behind me, I carry the pizza into the kitchen where Sophie has already gotten plates out of the cupboard. We each take a few slices, grab a couple of bottles of water, and head back into the living room to start the movie.

"Hold on a second," I say as I set my plate down on the small table I had set up in front of the couch earlier. "I'll be right back." I rush to the bedroom to grab the extra blankets that I had planned on putting out before I had received that phone call. Bringing the blankets back into the living room, I drape them over the back of the couch and smile at Sophie. "There—now if we get cold later, we have some extra blankets."

"Perfect," she says.

I sit down next to her and hit play on the Christmas movie I set up earlier.

"*Love Actually!* You remembered!"

"Of course I remember your favorite movie," I smile. "We used to watch it together every year."

We sit together and enjoy being close while we eat our food and watch. When we are finished eating, I pause the movie and take the dishes into the kitchen. When I return, I pull a blanket off of the back of the couch and wrap it around Sophie, pulling her into me before starting the movie again. She cuddles close and leans her head against my shoulder.

After the movie ends I ask, "Should we watch another?"

"Sure!" Sophie says excitedly. "You know I love Christmas movies. I would never pass up the chance to watch another one! What should we watch?"

I chuckle as I grab the remote to switch to a different movie. "I picked the first one, why don't you choose the next one?"

"Okay. How about *The Spirit of Christmas*? It's one of my new favorite Christmas movies."

"Sure, sounds good to me." I scroll through the list of movies until I find it. "You know, I don't even remember the last time I watched a Christmas movie."

"Really? You used to love watching them every year," she says as she pulls back to look at me.

"Yeah, I did—with you."

"Oh," Sophie says.

"After we broke up, I just couldn't bring myself to watch them anymore. Watching them reminded me too much of you and the movie nights we used to have."

"I'm sorry."

"No, there's nothing for you to apologize for Sophie. It's not your fault that I stopped watching them. Besides—I'm enjoying watching them again with you by my side, like it should be."

She leans up and gives me a kiss before snuggling back into my shoulder. I wrap the blanket around us tighter and put my arm around her before hitting play for the next movie.

At some point during the second movie, we must have both fallen asleep because as I blink my eyes open the sun is streaming in through the windows and into my eyes—it's morning. Sophie is still asleep on my shoulder. I kiss the top of her head and she sleepily opens her eyes to look up at me.

"We must really like sleeping in the living room," she laughs.

"Apparently," I say with a smile. "How about we try sleeping in a bedroom tonight?"

"That sounds nice—as long as we sleep in the same one. I like falling asleep with you."

"I wouldn't have it any other way," I tell her as I give her a kiss.

Sophie kisses me one more time and then sits up. "What should we do today? I want to go look at all of the ice sculptures tonight when they are finishing them up, but besides that I don't think anything else is going on."

"Is there anything specific that *you* want to do?" I ask.

Sophie gets a sly grin on her face before she looks at me and says, "Actually, yes, there is. All of that beautiful snow out there is calling my name. I just want to play in it like we used to when we were kids."

I burst out laughing. "You—you want to play in the snow?" I ask between gasps for air.

"Don't laugh at me!" she says between her own laughs. "I haven't played in the snow since we were kids. Being here and seeing all of this fluffy white snow makes me want to act like a kid again."

"I'm sorry. I didn't mean to laugh. It actually sounds like fun to me too. Sure, why not—let's do it!" We eat a quick breakfast, get dressed and put on all of our winter gear, and then head out the door for some fun in the snow.

SOPHIE

As soon as I open the door and step outside, the cold air hits my face. It's a beautiful sunny day, but the wind is chilly. I wrap my jacket more tightly around myself as Matt and I run into the giant back yard and flop down into the fluffy white snow. "Let's make snow angels!" I say excitedly. We both slide our legs in and out and our arms up and down to make the snow angels.

"Perfect!" Matt says as he stands and pulls me up from where I'm lying in the snow.

As he pulls me up I grab a fist full of snow and throw it down his shirt before I take off running and giggling.

"Shit! That's cold!" he shouts as he runs after me,

shaking the snow out of his shirt. "You're going to pay for that!"

As I'm running, I get hit in the back with a snowball. "That's the first of many!" Matt yells.

Reaching down, I scoop up another handful of snow and form it into a ball while still running. Turning around, I fire it straight at Matt—hitting him right in the chest. "Snowball fight!" I yell as I duck behind a nearby tree to hide while I gather up more ammunition.

With a snowball in hand I peek around the tree and see a snowball hurtling towards me. I pull back just in time before it hits the tree trunk and shatters into specks of snow.

I've formed a pile of snowballs next to me, ready for anything Matt can dish up. I take a chance to peer out again and throw one towards the direction the last snowball came from, hoping to draw him out into the open.

"Missed me!" Matt shouts as another one comes zooming past me.

We spend the next twenty minutes tossing snowballs at each other and dodging before I call a truce. Walking out from our hiding places Matt comes towards me with his hands in the air—showing me that he's honoring our truce and is unarmed. When he gets within reaching distance he lunges towards me and tackles me into the snow. We both go down into a heap, laughing so hard that tears are streaming down our faces. "I thought we had a truce?" I ask between giggles.

"I lied. I couldn't give up completely without getting *some* payback."

"Fair enough."

Matt pushes the hair out of my face as he kisses the tip of my nose. "What do you say about going inside to warm up?"

"Sounds good."

We make our way back inside and Matt lights a fire in the fireplace to warm up in front of. I head into the kitchen to make two cups of steaming hot chocolate.

"Need any help?" he asks as he comes into the kitchen.

"Nope. I've got it," I say, handing him one of the cups. "Here—this will help to warm us up."

Walking back into the living room we both take a seat in front of the fire. The warmth coming off of the flames feels like a blanket wrapping around me. "I didn't realize how cold it was out there until just now. That fire feels nice."

Matt smiles at me as he moves closer to wrap his

arm around me. "It's definitely a bit chilly out there. It was a lot of fun though."

"Especially when I got that snow down your shirt," I say with a chuckle.

"Yeah....*that*—not so much. That was freezing!"

"Oh, come on. It couldn't have been *that* bad. Remember that time when we were teenagers—we were swimming inside and you carried me outside and tossed me in the snow in my swimsuit? Now *that* was freezing!"

Matt starts to laugh. "I remember. You were so mad at me for that. I didn't think you were ever going to speak to me again."

"Yeah, well—I got over it pretty quickly. After you brought me a new fleece blanket and some flowers to apologize I couldn't stay mad at you."

"If only apologizing for everything were that easy."

I shake my head and grab his hand. "Don't Matt. Let's not bring up the past anymore, okay? Everything is going good between us again, let's not ruin it by dwelling on something we can't change."

"I'm sorry. I just can't help it. I still feel terrible for what I did. But I'll try to not bring it up anymore."

"Good. Now let's get back to enjoying this wonderful fire and our beautiful Christmas tree."

"Okay," Matt says as he brushes his lips across mine. "Let's enjoy—"

Whatever Matt was about to say is cut off by the sound of his cell phone buzzing.

"Just ignore that," he says as he nibbles at my ear and runs his fingers up and down my arms. "I'll check it later."

I turn to face him and crash my lips into his. Our tongues tangle as we deepen our kiss. He lays me down on the couch, kissing down my neck—and his phone rings again. Ignoring it, he grabs for the hem of my shirt to pull it off—and once again his phone rings.

"Damn it!" he shouts. "Give me a second to see what that's all about." He stomps into the bedroom where he left his phone. I can hear him cursing under his breath as he comes back into the living room.

"Who was that? Is everything alright?" I ask as I sit up on the couch.

"Everything's fine," he says angrily. He takes a deep breath in and then blows it out slowly. "I'm sorry. I shouldn't have snapped at you. It was nothing important—just a wrong number."

I look at him skeptically. "A wrong number called repeatedly?"

Closing his eyes and shaking his head he says, "I've been having trouble with someone calling me. I don't know—I guess someone they knew used to have this phone number or something. Nothing to worry about, okay?"

Something in his voice sounds off and I'm not sure that I believe his story, but I don't want to push him. I need to trust that if it's something important he will tell me about it. Too bad that I'm still working on trusting him again—otherwise I wouldn't be worrying about it right now, but I am scared he's hiding something, or someone, from me.

MATT

I should just tell Sophie about Victoria and not keep it a secret. Tell her that she's a crazy stalker that won't leave me alone and has delusions about us being in a relationship—which we most definitely are *not*. But I can't bring myself to do it. I don't want to ruin our Christmas and all of the happy times we've been having together by bringing up this problem with Victoria.

Victoria and I met just over a year ago when she moved to Chicago and started working in the university administration office. She has been trying to make us a couple ever since. Being the dean's daughter—and a member of the staff—she is always at the university functions that I attend and always tries to get close to me. She tries to attach herself to me when we attend the same staff mixers, grabbing onto my arm and batting her eyelashes to ask me to get her a cocktail. At work, she is always inserting herself into conversations I have with other professors and staff members so that she can stand as close as possible to me. She always seems to be hanging around the building during my office hours, waiting for my day to be over before purposely 'running into me' and hinting at things she would like to do on a date. I've tried to politely avoid her advances and let her know that I'm not interested, but she always threatens me by reminding me who my boss is. Victoria is daddy's little girl and I wouldn't put it past her to make up a story for her father that would get me into trouble.

I can't afford to lose my job, so I have to grit my teeth and deal with her at functions and work, but on my own personal time I do my best to ignore her. But she still doesn't seem to get it. I really should get a restraining order on her, but again—I'm afraid of her father and losing my job.

Bringing Sophie into this drama seems wrong. I made up the story about the wrong number that keeps calling me thinking it's someone else that used to have this number. I can only hope that she believes me and still trusts me through this little white lie.

Sophie is still sitting on the couch as I walk over to sit beside her. She still looks a little skeptical about my answer for the phone call, but hopefully I can make her forget about it. "Now—where were we?" I say, taking her hands in mine.

She sighs and shakes her head. "Sorry, Matt. The moment is somewhat ruined now. Besides—we need to get ready to head into town to look at those ice sculptures! They will be starting on the finishing touches pretty soon and that's my favorite part. We can't miss that!"

"Yeah, I guess you're right. Come on then, let's get ready," I say as I help pull her up off of the couch.

Sophie kisses me quickly and then goes to her bedroom to change into some warmer clothing. The weather outside has turned much colder since we had our adventure in the snow this afternoon, so I know the light sweater and jeans she had on earlier won't be warm enough. Neither will the light sweater I have on, so I go to my own room to throw on a sweatshirt over the top of a wool undershirt.

When I meet Sophie in the living room a few minutes later, she's now sporting her wool socks and a sweatshirt that I recognize as my old one from high school over a wool undershirt, and I can't help but laugh. "You still have that old thing? I thought you would have burned it or something after I left."

She looks at the floor sheepishly. "I thought about burning it, but I just couldn't do it. It's so warm and it has always been one of my favorites since I stole it from you at that football game in high school."

"Well I'm glad you didn't destroy it. I still like seeing you wear it. And, just for the record, you didn't *steal* it—I wanted you to have it."

"I'm glad I kept it. It has always reminded me of you and the good times we had together. Now it can be a part of our new memories," she says as she smiles at me.

"Definitely. Now come on, let's go make more new memories together." Grabbing her coat and boots I hand them to her before shrugging my own jacket on and slipping into my boots.

On the drive into town we talk about what we think the ice sculptures will look like this year. "Do you have any ideas about what we'll see tonight?" I ask.

"Hmm—I'm not sure. I've been trying to guess what some of the month-long sculptures are under the tarps that have been covering them, but I haven't been able to figure any of them out. For the all-nighters—maybe some reindeer or snowmen? What do you think?"

"I have absolutely no idea," I laugh. "I was never any good at guessing them before they were revealed."

The event started over fifty years ago when one of the shop owners decided to carve an ice sculpture for a decoration in front of his store. Everyone loved it and more shop owners started to do the same. Crowds would form to admire all of the sculptures. Over the years townspeople started to join in and it eventually became a yearly event. Every year the town comes up with a different theme for them and this year's theme is "Christmas Traditions". The sculptures line the main street in front of the businesses—where they have been carved in advance—and also the town square where the participants started working on them last night and will be finishing up their carvings tonight.

When we arrive, I find a spot to park—not too far away from the event. Sophie and I make our way to main street, walking hand in hand. We stop to gaze at all of the wonderful creations along the way to the town square.

"They're all so beautiful this year!" Sophie

exclaims as we pass by a stunning sculpture of Santa's workshop in front of the toy store.

"They really are. I forgot how impressive these sculptures can get."

"Look at how detailed they are! There are even little name tags on the reindeer harnesses," she says as she points to a sculpture of Santa's reindeer pulling a sleigh. "I can't wait to see the all-night ones in the town square."

As we walk down the street we pass each of the businesses with sculptures near their entrances. They all have ice carved to fit the "Christmas Traditions" theme perfectly: a family table and chairs made of ice complete with a Christmas dinner set out on it in front of the grocery store, a grand ice piano surrounded by ice carolers in front of the music store, and an airplane surrounded by icy palm trees in front of the travel agency.

In the town square there are people everywhere watching the carvers finish up their masterpieces. Sophie squeals and claps her hands together. "I feel like a little kid on Christmas morning! I forgot how much I've missed this."

I chuckle and kiss the top of her head as we continue to watch the carvers put on the finishing touches. "It's amazing what these carvers can do with a block of ice," I say as we gaze at the beautiful designs—ice skaters, people building a snowman, people sledding and skiing, and even a mini Eiffel Tower with people holding a sign that says "Family Vacation".

Next to me I hear Sophie sniffle. I glance over towards her and see tears shimmering in her eyes. "What's wrong, Sophie?"

She gives me a half smile. "Sorry. Don't mind me. The Eiffel Tower just reminds me that my sister is there right now and I miss her."

"I'm sorry. Have you talked to her lately? Maybe you can video call her when we get back to the cabin."

"No, she's six hours ahead of us, it will be too late to call her tonight. Maybe I can video call her tomorrow though. I can't wait to tell her all about the sculptures and how you and I visited the Eiffel Tower in its miniature ice form. We should take a selfie in front of it so I can send it to her."

"Sure, that's a great idea!" Sophie hands me her phone and I wrap an arm around her before taking the picture and handing her phone back to her.

She turns around to take another look at the sculpture in front of us. "It really is beautiful."

I hate seeing Sophie sad so I try to cheer her up

by changing the topic. "So, out of all of the sculptures we saw tonight, which one is your favorite?"

"Oh wow. You want me to choose *one*? But they are all so amazing!"

"Yep, just one. I have mine picked out already," I say with a smile.

"Hmmm." She taps her finger to her mouth while she thinks about it. "I would have to say my favorite is the people sledding because it makes me remember the sled races we had together."

"That's a good choice! *My* favorite is the ice skaters."

"Any particular reason why?" she asks.

I wrap my arms around her and pull her close. I can feel her warm breath as her face is inches away from mine. "Because it reminds me of the night we got back together." I brush my lips against hers and whisper, "And because it reminds me of the night you made me feel whole again. I love you, Sophie."

"I love you too, Matt."

As she kisses me we hear the familiar voices of Trisha and Callie. Trisha is teasingly singing "Sophie and Matt, sitting in a tree. K-I-S-S-I-N-G!"

"Awwww! I *knew* you two would work it out," Callie says.

Sophie and I both start laughing as we pull apart.

"What are you—ten?" she jokingly asks Trisha. "Hi, Callie. I guess you *were* right after all."

"Of course I was right," says Callie with a smile.

"What did you two think of the ice sculptures this year?" asks Trisha.

"They were amazing!" I say. "Hard to believe that they all started off as giant blocks of ice."

"They were all gorgeous!" says Sophie.

"Still one of my favorite parts of the holiday celebration," Callie chimes in.

We visit with the two of them for a few more minutes before making our way to my truck to go back to the cabin. "Did you have a good time?" I ask.

"Yes, I did. Did you?"

"Definitely, but now I'm ready to fall asleep with you in my arms tonight."

"Sounds wonderful," she says dreamily.

A few minutes later we arrive at the cabin and go inside for the night. After getting ready, we snuggle close together in my bed, wrapped warmly in the fluffy blankets and each other's arms. "Goodnight, Sophie." When there is no response I realize that she has already fallen asleep. I smile to myself as I wrap my arms tighter around her and close my eyes to drift off to sleep.

SOPHIE

I wake up to the sound of wind howling outside the windows. The room is still bathed in darkness instead of the usual morning sunlight. Matt's arm is still wrapped around me as he sleeps soundly at my side. Reaching for my phone on the nightstand, I pick it up to check the time and can't believe I slept so late. It's eight-thirty. How strange. Why is it still so dark?

I slide gently out from under Matt's arm and crawl out of bed. "Where are you going?" he mumbles.

"Sorry. I didn't mean to wake you. It's morning—I was just going to go to the bathroom and then make some coffee."

"It can't be morning. It still looks like the middle of the night."

"I know. The wind is really blowing out there; maybe something blew over and is blocking the window."

Matt crawls out of bed and follows me out into the hallway. After a quick stop at the bathroom we walk into the living room to look out the windows.

"Oh, wow!" Matt says as he looks over my shoulder toward the big kitchen windows.

"What?" I ask as I turn to see what he's looking at. I gasp as I see what he's pointing at. The windows are almost completely blocked by snow. Through the small sliver still visible at the top, we can see the snow swirling as the wind whips around violently. Sometime during the night a blizzard started and now we are snowed in. "Well that's not good."

We make our way over to the entryway to peer out the front window. It's equally buried in snow. "Looks like we will be staying inside today," Matt chuckles. "We'll have to call someone to come dig us out later when the snow stops. Doesn't look like that will be happening anytime soon though. We'll have to find something to keep us occupied." He winks at me and grins.

"Is that all you think about?" I ask as I roll my eyes.

"Hey, can you blame me? We're making up for lost time."

"Fair enough," I say with a giggle, "but let's find something else to do too. We can't stay in bed *all* day. I'm sure Rachel and David have some board games or something around here."

"Who said anything about staying in bed? There's a whole house to explore!" Matt exclaims.

I roll my eyes again. "Come on—let's search for some board games."

We search through the cabin, opening cabinets and drawers, until we find some games stashed on a shelf in the back of a closet. There are enough games to keep us entertained until the afternoon at least.

"Why don't you let me pick out a game for us and call for someone to dig us out, since we can't even open the door, while you go video chat with your sister?" Matt asks. "I know you miss her. Since we are stuck here, today is the perfect opportunity for you to call her and catch up."

"You don't mind?"

"Of course not."

"Ok, thanks." I leave Matt to pick out a game and head to my bedroom to get my laptop. Opening it, I click on the video call icon and select my sister from my favorites. She answers almost immediately and I smile when I see her face on my screen—the same blonde hair and green eyes looking back at me, sitting in a comfy chair in her room at her host family's home.

"Hey, sis! How are you? Where are you? Are you having a good Christmas break so far? Are you still in pajamas?" Jessica asks.

I laugh at Jessica's rapid fire questions. "Hi, Jessica! So many questions!"

"Sorry—I miss my big sister!"

"It's alright. And to answer your questions—I'm great, I'm at a cabin in Winterglen, I'm *definitely* having a good break so far and yes I'm in pajamas; it's still morning here."

"Oh, right. I forgot about the time difference," she says with a shrug. "You went to Winterglen for Christmas? That's awesome! I haven't really been there since we moved. Is Callie's Diner still there and does the town still have the really cool celebration?"

"Yeah, Callie's Diner is still here. I've been there a few times already actually. She still has the best hot chocolate around and *duh* they still have the celebration. That's part of the reason I came back here.

Matt and I have been going to all of the events and having a blast!"

She raises her eyebrow and looks at me in astonishment. "Matt? Matt who? As in *the* Matt who broke your heart right after high school?"

I let out a sigh. "Yes—*that* Matt. We—got back together." Jessica scowls at me and crosses her arms. "Don't give me that look, Jess."

"You can't be serious about taking that jerk back! What are you thinking, Sophie?! How did you even meet up with him again?"

"The cabin I'm renting belongs to my friend Rachel. Her husband didn't realize that *she* rented it to me and *he* rented it to Matt. There's nowhere else available to stay right now because of the celebration so we agreed to share the cabin—and things just kind of went from there. We talked and he told me why he broke up with me and admitted that he never really wanted to."

"And you believe him?" Jessica asks in disbelief.

"I do. When we first agreed to share the cabin I told him I would only agree to be friends, nothing more. But while we have been enjoying all of the events together and are getting to know each other again, things have changed. I truly believe that he *does* love me and I have never really stopped loving him. It wouldn't be fair to either of us if I didn't give him a second chance."

"But what about *after* Christmas? Are you just going to do long-distance when you go back to your life in Chicago?"

"No—we don't have to. He lives in Chicago, too."

"Well that's convenient," she replies sarcastically as she rolls her eyes at me.

"Don't worry, everything will be fine this time. Things are going well for the most part."

"What do you mean for the most part?"

"It's nothing. He's received some phone calls that he acts really strange after answering or listening to the voicemails, but I don't think it's anything to worry about."

"Sophie," she starts to say before I cut her off.

"Don't say it. I'll be fine. Now enough about me—how's Paris?"

She gives me a worried look, but drops it and answers my question. "It's fantastic! I absolutely love it here. My host family is amazing and they have been showing me all around. I've seen all of the usual tourist attractions like the Eiffel Tower and the Louvre Museum, of course, but they have also taken me to some other not so well-known sites."

"That sounds so cool. What are these other sites?"

"Well, let's see," Jessica says as she taps her cheek. "They've taken me to the Catacombs of Paris, which were really creepy. The site was set up to help solve the problem of the cemeteries being full." She shivers and makes a face at the memory. "But it's a really popular site. We waited for two hours to get in! Oh, and they took me to the Montmartre Vineyards which were really beautiful. It's over eight hundred years old and is the last active vineyard in the whole city."

"Wow! It sounds like you are having a wonderful time," I say smiling at her.

"I really am! Wish you could be here, though." Jessica says as she makes a pouty face.

"Nah—you wouldn't want your big sister cramping your style. I have to know though, how *is* Paris at Christmas? I've always thought it would be beautiful."

"It really is! The city is lit up with *so* many lights. There are Christmas markets set up everywhere and the department store windows go all out with decorations. I think my favorite things so far have been seeing the Eiffel Tower all lit up and ice skating at the Grand Palais. The rink is set up under this beautiful glass dome—it feels magical."

"I'm really happy for you, Jess. I'm glad you're

having such a great time. One of the ice sculptures here in town was the Eiffel Tower at Christmas and it made me think of you. I miss you."

"The ice sculpture sounds awesome. Send me some pictures if you took any! I miss you too, sis."

"We took a selfie in front of it. I'll send it to you when we hang up."

"Sounds great! Send any other pictures you have too!"

"Ok, I will, but I better let you go. Matt and I are snowed in and we are going to play some board games. He's probably waiting for me. Besides, you probably have *something* you could be doing that's more fun than talking to me."

"Nah," Jessica says with a grin. "Seriously though, just be careful okay? I don't want to see you hurt again, Sophie."

"Don't worry, I'll be careful. Love you, sis!"

"Love you, too! Bye!" Jessica waves and blows me a kiss through the screen.

I blow a kiss back to her before ending our call and putting my laptop away. I really needed that call with my sister. I'm glad I was able to talk to her and see her smiling face. My vacation will be a little more enjoyable knowing that she's alright. Now it's time to go see which game Matt has picked out.

MATT

I hear Sophie coming out of her bedroom as I'm finishing setting up the game. I've started a wood fire in the fireplace and put some of those colorful pinecones that she likes so much into it. The fire roars to life as it sparks with beautiful blue and green colors from the pinecones. With the Christmas tree lights on, it looks perfect for an afternoon with Sophie. Cushions are arranged on the floor in front of the fire along with blankets and the game board sitting in the center. A small table with snacks—cheese bites, crackers, and apple slices—is set up off to the side.

"Wow! It looks very festive in here!" she exclaims with a smile as she enters the room. "What game are we playing?"

"Domination," I say with a grin. "I remember it always used to be your favorite."

"Still is! I play it with my family every time we get together," she says as she starts jumping up and down and swinging her arms around like a boxer getting ready for a match.

"What are you *doing?*" I say as I let out a deep belly laugh.

Smirking at me she says, "I have to get ready to kick your ass. You know, loosen up and clear my mind so I can concentrate."

"You're ridiculous, you know that?" I say still laughing.

"Ha! You won't think I'm ridiculous when you're losing. Now let's do this!" Sophie flops down onto one of the cushions and sits cross-legged. "I want to be the Shiba Inu, which piece do you want?"

"I'll be the electric car." Sophie hands me the electric car as I take a seat on the other cushion.

"Let's roll to see who goes first," Sophie says as she rolls a die. "Three! Your turn."

I shake the die in my hand and blow on it before letting it drop with a thud on the board. "Ha! I rolled a five! I go first."

"Enjoy your 'win' because that's the only one you're getting today."

"Oh, you think so, do you?" I tease.

"Yes, yes I do," Sophie says confidently, popping one of the cheese bites into her mouth. "We should make this a little more interesting—maybe play *strip* Domination?"

"Strip Domination?" I asks raising my eyebrows. "How does that work?"

"How about every time one of us lands on a property of which the other person owns a complete set, the one who landed on it loses an article of clothing?"

"Sounds fair enough," I say with a grin. "Get ready to strip."

We take turns rolling the dice, buying properties, and building hotels for the next hour and a half. Sophie has collected the majority of the properties and I have lost the majority of my clothing. Taking the dice in my hand I shake and blow on them for luck before letting them drop to the board. I move my electric car the number of spaces and land on Beverly Hills which is owned by Sophie—and of course she has a hotel on it. "I don't suppose you want to cut me a break on rent?" I ask as I make a sad face.

"Not a chance! That's two-thousand dollars. Pay up!" she says happily. "And lose the boxers."

Handing over the last of my money, and stripping out of my boxers, I say, "That's it—I'm out. You win."

"Ha! Yes! Told you I could still kick your ass!" she says grinning at me. "Good game!" She offers her hand to me for a handshake.

"Good game," I say as I take her hand in mine. Instead of shaking her hand, I tighten my grip and gently pull her toward me to give her a kiss.

"What's next?" she mumbles against my lips.

"What do *you* want to do next? I picked the first game."

"That depends—how long do we have until someone digs us out of here? I forgot to ask before we started playing."

"We have a while. We aren't the only ones who were snowed in last night and we're pretty far down on the list to be shoveled out. It'll be *at least* a couple more hours."

"In that case, I think we should have a little *fun* before we play another game. After all, you're already naked." Sophie pushes the game board out of the way and climbs over onto my lap, wrapping her legs around my waist. Cupping my face in-between her hands, she covers my mouth with her own.

I part her lips with my tongue, tasting her, as she

moans into my mouth. My fingers tangle in her silky hair as I deepen the kiss. Lying back, I pull her down with me so that her body is blanketing mine. Rocking my hips up into hers, I smile against her lips as she gasps.

Reaching into the pocket of my discarded pajama pants, I pull out a condom as she slowly pushes her own pajama pants down, wiggling out of them. She rips open the condom and rolls it onto me. "Are you in a hurry?" I tease as I chuckle.

"Mmm-hmm," Sophie mutters as she kisses me and slides down onto my hard length, making me groan.

"No complaints here," I pant as I gently hold her hips to move her up and down.

Her hands grip my shoulders as I thrust up into her, slowly at first, picking up speed with each thrust.

"You feel so good," she murmurs as I kiss down her neck.

Slowing my thrusts, I tangle my legs with hers and flip us, so that I'm on top. I push her pajama top up and graze my fingers along her stomach and up her sides. Sophie shivers in anticipation as my hands move towards her nipples. I gently massage her breasts as I push into her again. We move together in a steady rhythm, panting and moaning, until we are both crying out with our release.

Slowly, I roll off of her and dispose of the condom before pulling her close. "Have I told you lately how much I love you, Sophie?"

She smiles up at me. "Not lately."

"Well I *do*."

"I love you, too, Matt. I'm so glad that we ended up stuck here together—that we've been given a second chance."

"Me too. It's been the best Christmas I've had in a while."

My cell phone rings and I get up to answer it, hoping that it's not my stalker. Checking the screen, I see that it's a local number and answer it.

"Hello?"

"Hi, could I speak to Matt, please?" says a friendly female voice on the other end.

"This is Matt."

"Hi, Matt. This is Amy from the Frosty Snow Removal Company. I was just calling to give you an update. We should have a driver out to your location to start clearing snow in about two hours."

"Perfect! Thank you."

"You're welcome. Have a wonderful day."

"You too." I end the call and walk back in by

Sophie who has put her pajama pants back on, and is sitting watching the colorful flames dance in the fireplace.

"Who was that?" she asks.

"The snow removal company," I say as I pick my pants up off of the floor where they had been discarded and pull them on. "They should be here in about two hours."

"Great! That should give us enough time to play another game or two, but let's eat first. I'm starving! Cheese and crackers only holds me for so long," she smiles.

Sophie heads into the kitchen as I quickly follow behind her. As I start to walk towards the refrigerator she stops me. "I'll make lunch. You've cooked for me already, now it's my turn to cook for you."

"You—you're going to cook for me?" I gulp with a worried expression on my face. The last time Sophie had tried cooking for me I had gotten food poisoning. Granted that was back in high school, but still. It's not something I'd like to relive.

Sophie lets out a laugh. "Calm down. I'm not going to make you sick. I *did* learn how to cook, you know. Just like you, I had to learn when I went off to college."

"Okay. You make lunch." I take a seat at the table

where I can see her. I watch as she takes ingredients out of the refrigerator and wait nervously as Sophie prepares food. My stomach is queasy at the memory of last time, but she seems really excited to cook. Hopefully I don't regret this decision.

SOPHIE

I'm still chuckling to myself at the look on Matt's face as I pull ingredients out of the refrigerator. He's sitting at the kitchen table watching me with such a cautious expression. "I promise—I won't make you sick again," I say reassuringly.

"You know, I'm really not that hungry after all. Maybe I'll just have a banana or something." Matt says.

"Matt," I say as I set the ingredients on the counter and put my hands on my hips. "You'll be fine. Quit being such a baby."

"I'm not being a baby. I'm just worried about my stomach. I don't feel like spending the rest of the day throwing up," he says with a queasy expression on his face.

"I said I was sorry about last time," I say. "But I've come a long way since then. Believe me—you'll be fine."

"Well—okay. I believe you," he says nervously.

"Really? Because you sound like you *don't* believe me," I tease as I pull out a couple of pots and pans, and place them on the stove.

"No, I do. Just not sure if my stomach does."

"Well, I'll just have to prove it." I dice some tomatoes and the onion that I grabbed from the refrigerator before tossing them into a blender to purée. Transferring the mixture to the pot on the stove, I add the tomato-vegetable juice cocktail along with some salt and pepper.

While I wait for that to boil I get started on sandwiches. "What are you making?" Matt asks, craning his neck to see over the counter from where he sits. "I need to prepare my stomach for whatever you dish up."

"Comfort food," I smile.

"Comfort food to whom?" Matt says slyly.

I ignore the comment as I give him a stare and a smile. "Since we're snowed in, I figured I would make tomato soup and grilled cheese sandwiches."

"Yum! You remember my favorite meal," he says with a grin. "But I usually just settle for soup from a can."

"I wanted to make something special since you made *my* favorite meal that first night we were here. Besides, this is just a simple soup recipe. Not much to it. Maybe I can teach it to you sometime. I use a secret ingredient that makes it taste fantastic."

"I would really like that. Is there anything I can do to help?" he asks.

The sandwiches are in the pan, and the soup is simmering. "You could set the table if you want."

"That I can do," Matt says as he grabs the plates, bowls, and silverware from the cabinet.

A few minutes later and the food is almost done. "Sophie, it smells *amazing* in here!"

"Good, because everything is ready to eat. Let's dish it up," I say. I bring the sandwiches and the soup to the table where Matt is sitting.

"I'm looking forward to trying it," Matt says as I pour a few ladles full of soup into his bowl.

"Well, now you'll just have to see how it tastes!"

"I'm sure it's wonderful—and my stomach is prepared," Matt says with a wink. Regardless of his enthusiasm, the bite he takes from his soup is still tentative. "Oh—well—this *does* taste amazing!"

"Thanks," I say with a laugh after swallowing my own mouthful of food. "I'm glad you like it."

"You know, I don't think I've had tomato soup in years—certainly not homemade. Nor a grilled cheese sandwich for that matter," he says as he takes another bite.

"You haven't eaten your favorite meal in years? Why not?"

"I don't know. I guess it reminded me too much of the times we had together. Every time I would eat it, I would think of those snowy days when school was cancelled—when you would come over to my house and my mom would make it for us."

"Yeah, I know what you mean. I hadn't eaten Chicken Parmesan until that night you made it for me again. I tried a couple of times, but all I could think about was your mom making it for me when we would have our movie nights. I just couldn't stand to eat it anymore."

"Well, then, I'm glad I made it and you were able to enjoy your favorite meal again," he says as he takes one last bite of grilled cheese.

"Me too. And I'm glad I was able to make yours as well." I finish the last of my soup and stand up to clear the table.

"No, let me. You cooked," Matt says as he takes the dishes out of my hands.

"Thanks. Do you want to play another game since we still have a little while before the snow removal company arrives?"

"Sure. Why don't you go choose something while I do the dishes?" he asks.

"Okay." I leave Matt in the kitchen and walk over to where we stacked the games in the living room. Looking through the options, I narrow it down to either Scrabble or the deck of cards. Choosing Scrabble out of the pile, I carry it over to the cozy spot in front of the fire where we played Domination earlier.

Matt walks into the living room a few minutes later and sits down next to me on one of the cushions. "Oooh, Scrabble. I'm a master at this one. You're going down this time," he teases.

"We'll see about that. I'm kind of a whiz at it myself," I say.

We set up the game board and shake the bag of letters to mix them up before each choosing our tiles. "I went first last time, so you go first this time," Matt says.

I search my tiles to find my first word. "D-E-A-L-T," I spell out as I lay the letters down. "Dealt.

That's six points, plus double word score, so twelve points."

"Not bad. Good starter word," Matt says. "Now let's see what I've got." He searches through his letters to see what word he can make. "D-E-E-R. That's two, three, six—since this E is on a triple letter square—seven points."

We continue making words, Matt pulling into the lead, until we hear a rumble coming from outside. We both scramble over to the window by the entrance to see if we can see anything. Slowly, bits of light are beginning to stream through from the headlights as the plow carefully pushes snow out of the way and shovelers remove the snow closer to the house. The sun has already started to set and it's starting to get dark outside due to being that time of year.

"We're saved!" I say excitedly, grinning at Matt.

"Don't think this means we're not finishing our game—I'm winning right now and I'm not letting you off that easy!" he says with a laugh. I pout my lips and bat my eyelashes at him. "Don't even think about it."

Letting out a sigh and shrugging, I say, "It was worth a shot."

We watch from the window as the workers

continue to tackle the pile of snow in front of the cabin door. It seems like they have been digging for hours when one of them finally knocks on the door. Matt pulls it open slowly. "Hey there Matt and Sophie," says the company owner—who happens to be Tom—as he nods in our direction. "Sorry it took so long to get you out. We've been pretty busy all day."

"No problem. You're secretary, Amy, called a couple of hours ago to let us know that you had a lot of calls, but you would be here soon," Matt says.

"Yeah, that blizzard last night really did a number on the town. Especially those of you that are farther out," says Tom.

"Thanks for digging us out," I say. "We really appreciate it."

"No problem. That's what we do."

"How much do we owe you?" Matt asks.

"Don't worry about it," Tom says waving a hand. "We're not charging anybody today. Consider it a Christmas gift."

"Are you sure?" I ask in shock.

"Yes, I'm sure. Have a Merry Christmas! Hope to see you two at the Christmas Eve dance!"

"We'll be there!" I say with a smile.

We wave goodbye to Tom and the other men

before Matt closes the door. "Well, that was very nice of them to not charge us," Matt says.

I shake my head. "It really was. That definitely wouldn't happen in the city."

"No, you're right about that. I guess that's one of the reasons I love being back here in Winterglen. Everyone is so nice and friendly."

"I've been enjoying being back here as well. It's nice taking a vacation from all of the hustle and bustle of Chicago. Plus, I've had a lot of fun participating in all of the events and seeing my friends again. Speaking of events—we should go to the village market tomorrow to do some shopping. I still need to get a gift for you."

"Sophie, you don't need to buy anything for me."

"Yes, I do. I *want* to." I smile at Matt and give him a quick kiss on the lips.

"Shopping at the market sounds good to me. I still have to get *your* gift, too."

"Good. It's settled then. We'll go shopping tomorrow. For now, I think I'll go back to my room to read," I say as I start trying to sneak down the hallway to my bedroom.

"Oh no you don't!" Matt laughs as he catches my hand and pulls me back. "We still have a game to finish." He wraps me in his arms and kisses the tip of my nose.

"Alright, alright. Let's go," I say reluctantly. "Maybe my luck will turn around again. You never know—I could still win."

"Not likely," Matt teases, wiggling his eyebrows. "But you can try."

We make our way back to our Scrabble game in front of the fire to finish playing. In the end, Matt wins by a landslide.

"Great game, Matt."

"Thanks. You put up a good fight," he says smiling.

"Thanks, I tried."

We clean up our game and put it in the pile with the rest of the games before putting them all back in the closet where we found them. Looking at the clock, it's already pretty late. Matt and I decide that since we've already been having fun inside all day we may as well stay here. I call to order us a pizza for dinner while Matt finds a Christmas movie to watch and we spend the rest of the night cuddling by the fire.

MATT

Sophie and I make our way to the Christmas village market to do our last minute shopping for each other. There are vendors spread out all around the town square selling their various crafts and trinkets. Several of the local shops also have booths set up to make it more convenient for their customers to do all of their shopping in one location.

Since I am shopping for Sophie and she is shopping for me we decide it's best to split up and meet somewhere when we are finished. "How about you go do your shopping and I'll do mine and we'll meet at the Christmas tree in the center in about half an hour?"

"Sounds good to me. I'll start in this direction and you start in that direction."

"Works for me. I'll see you in half an hour." I give her a quick kiss and wave goodbye.

Sophie waves as she strolls off towards the far end of the market to start her shopping. I make my way to the booths closest to me to browse through their goods. I'm not exactly sure yet what I want to get for Sophie, but I know that I will know it when I see it. I walk past booths with vendors selling handcrafted hats and scarves, vendors selling small intricately detailed wooden figurines depicting holiday themed scenes and items, and others with beautifully painted artwork. Nothing really catches my eye until I come across the booth with the jewelry. Displayed in the center of the table is a beautifully crafted charm bracelet featuring shiny silver snowflakes with crystal accents, a silver sleigh, and a pair of glittery ice skates.

"Hi! Is there anything specific you are looking for today? Anything you'd like to see closer?" the vendor asks.

"Could I please see this bracelet?" I ask, pointing to the charm bracelet.

"Of course. Very good choice." The lady smiles at

me as she hands it over for me to look at more closely. "Buying it for anyone special?"

"Yes, actually. My girlfriend." Turning the bracelet around in my hand I inspect all of the little details. The snowflake reminds me of our snowball fight and of course the sleigh and the ice skates remind me of the night that Sophie kissed me for the first time in ages. It was the night that she *truly* let me back into her life. "It's perfect! I'll take it," I tell the vendor.

"Excellent! Would you like me to wrap this up for you?"

"Yes, please. Thank you!" A few minutes later I am walking towards the tree carrying my beautifully wrapped gift for Sophie.

Standing next to the tree I glance around to see if I can spot Sophie. I see her walking towards me with a gift in her hand. Suddenly I hear a familiar voice calling my name and I spin in the direction it's coming from, horrified to see Victoria sprinting towards me.

"There you are my love!" Victoria exclaims as she flings her arms around my neck and crushes her lips to mine.

Out of the corner of my eye I see a flash of

Sophie's heartbroken face as she turns and dashes away in the other direction. I want to run after her, but I know that I need to deal with Victoria first. It's time that I face this ridiculous drama and end it once and for all.

I untangle Victoria's arms from around my neck, pushing her away as I angrily ask, "What the hell Victoria? What are you doing here? And how did you find me?"

"Oh, I have my ways," she says sweetly. "Besides, it's pretty easy to find you when you leave notes lying around. Even if they *are* cryptic. I just had to do a little digging on the internet to figure out what they meant."

My mind races trying to think of what notes she could possibly be talking about. I was careful not to tell anyone where I was going so that they wouldn't accidentally let it slip. I did jot down the name and phone number for David, the cabin owner, when I first found the listing. But I *know* I shoved that piece of paper along with the name of Mr. Elliott's hardware store for picking up the key into the back of my planner in a locked desk drawer in my office. Looking back, I should have destroyed the papers after I transferred all of the information into my cell phone, but I saved them just in case and had completely forgotten about them until now. They were shoved where no one except me should have been able to find them. Damn, I should have destroyed them. "How the hell did you see those notes? They were stashed inside my personal planner, inside of a *locked* desk drawer, in my office which was also locked. And how did those give away where I was—they literally had names and phone numbers on them."

"There aren't a whole lot of listings in the yellow pages for a Mr. Elliott's with that phone number, you know. All I had to do was search for it to see where it was located." Victoria smiles at me and bats her eyelashes as she says, "As for how I got into your office, well, if daddy's little girl asks for the keys to your office to retrieve something that I left in there when we were—you know—then he gives them to me." I stare at her in disbelief. "Once I was in there I just looked around until I found something useful—which I did when I broke into your desk. I just *had* to find you. I wasn't about to let you spend Christmas *alone*. What kind of girlfriend would that make me if I didn't spend the holidays with you?" she says as she tries to wrap her arms around my neck again.

"Victoria!" I shout as I push her off, "We are not,

and have never been, together! You're *not* my girlfriend! Why can't you get that through your head? That's why I avoid all of your phone calls. That's why I came here to get away and be alone. Staying far away from you—that was the whole point!"

"Honestly, Matt," she huffs. "You can't *really* mean that. We're perfect together."

"No, Victoria! I've told you a thousand times that I'm not interested. My heart belongs to someone else. That's never going to change. Now leave me alone or I will get a restraining order."

The look on Victoria's face turns to one of hate. If looks could kill, then I would be dead. "I'm going to tell daddy. He will fire you! You will never work in Chicago again! Are you absolutely sure you want to treat me this way? Ruin your career? Ruin your life?"

"I really don't care at this point if your father *does* fire me. I don't even care if he makes it so that I can't work in the state of Illinois anymore. I just want *you* out of my life. Now leave!"

As Victoria storms off, I run to find Sophie. My conversation with Victoria only took a few minutes, but it feels like it has been an eternity. I know Sophie saw Victoria kissing me and I need to finally tell her the truth about what has been going on. I can only hope that she will forgive me for not telling her sooner and believe me when I explain about the kiss.

Looking everywhere, I don't see Sophie anywhere in the shopping village. I run a hand through my hair as my eyes frantically scan the crowd, hoping to catch a glimpse of her *somewhere*. Suddenly a nearby vendor—a man I recognize, but can't place at the moment—says, "Hey, Matt. Are you looking for Sophie?"

"Yes! Have you seen her?"

"I sure did," he says shaking his head. "Poor thing ran that way crying. She jumped into a taxi and headed back towards her rental cabin. You just missed her."

"Shit!" I turn to leave calling, "Thanks!" over my shoulder as I sprint to my truck and race back to the cabin.

When I arrive at the cabin I slam my truck into park and jump out, rushing to get inside. I find Sophie angrily packing her belongings. Tears are streaming down her cheeks, clothes are thrown haphazardly into her suitcase, and she is slamming drawers closed as she gathers the last of her toiletries. Finally she picks up her laptop and shoves it into her bag. "Sophie. What are you doing?" I ask gently. I swallow around the lump in my throat, panicking at the thought that I've lost her.

"I'm packing! What does it look like I'm doing?" Sophie yells.

"Please don't leave. Please let me explain," I beg.

"Save it, Matt! I don't want to hear it. I can't believe I trusted you again. Clearly I didn't learn my lesson the first time. I let you back into my life and you've broken my heart for a second time. I *knew* something was up with all of those phone calls you've been receiving. I just didn't realize that the calls made you angry because they threatened your secret—that you already have a girlfriend! Or hell, maybe even a wife! It wasn't enough for you that you broke me the first time—you had to go and make me the *other woman*?" She slams her suitcase shut, zips it, and pushes past me to the door.

"Sophie, please! It's not like that! Just talk to me for a minute," I plead as I follow her out of the room.

"Goodbye, Matt," she says sadly as she walks out the door, slamming it behind her.

I stand in the entrance, tears welling in my eyes and cursing at both Victoria and myself. If it wasn't for her showing up, everything would have been fine. But some of the blame is on me—I should have told Sophie the truth about the phone calls immediately. That I have a stalker. Then maybe this wouldn't have happened. Maybe I wouldn't be feeling like I just blew my second chance at happiness with the woman I love. How the hell am I going to fix this with Sophie? *Can* I fix it?

SOPHIE

I throw my suitcase into my car and fall into the driver's seat. Quickly wiping the tears out of my eyes, I turn the key in the ignition, put the car in reverse, and back out of my parking spot. Without even glancing back, I throw the car into drive and speed away from Matt and the cabin. It was the place that should have been part of my happiest Christmas memories and the place that reminded me of how Matt and I rekindled our relationship. Now it's the place that will haunt my nightmares for being the worst Christmas ever.

What am I supposed to do now? I *could* make the couple hour drive back to Chicago, I guess, but I don't think I'm really in any condition to do so. The hot tears are still burning my eyes and clouding my vision, making it hard to see to drive. My heart feels like it has been ripped out of my chest and stomped on repeatedly. Taking a deep breath, I decide to go to Callie's Diner to drink some of her comforting hot chocolate and figure out what to to next.

After parking my car I make my way inside and slowly trudge to the counter. I order my drink and take a seat in a booth by the window while I wait for it to be ready. Staring out the window—not really seeing anything—I don't even realize that my name has been called for my hot chocolate until someone sets it down in front of me. Glancing up, I see Trisha standing next to my table with a concerned expression on her face. "Thanks. I didn't hear my name called," I say with a shaky voice as I look down at my hands.

"Sophie, what's wrong?" Trisha asks as she sits down across from me.

"Matt's an asshole and I feel *so* stupid," I reply miserably.

"You're *not* stupid. What happened? What did he do?"

I swirl the steaming liquid around in my cup, still not able to meet Trisha's eyes. "Earlier at the

Christmas market I—I saw him kissing another woman. And I heard her call him *my love*."

"Oh, I see," she says with concern in her voice.

"Oh yeah. She was all over him. After everything that happened after high school—I thought we could move past it. I thought we could make it work this time. I thought he still loved me, but I guess I was wrong. Apparently I was just a piece of ass on the side to keep him company for Christmas. I feel like such an idiot for trusting him again." Fresh tears are streaming down my face as Trisha leans over the table to give me a hug.

"It'll be alright, Sophie."

"Whatever. It's over now," I say shaking my head. "I can't stay at the cabin with him anymore, though. I just can't."

"Where will you go?"

"Home, I guess. Drive through the night if I have to. I don't know where else *to* go."

"Sophie. I can't let you do that. I don't want my best friend to be alone at Christmas. Especially not with a broken heart. Why don't you come and stay with me? My house is full of out-of-town relatives, but I have a comfy pull-out couch in my den that you can sleep on."

"No, I can't. I don't want to impose and you don't

want me moping around, ruining your holiday with my crappy mood."

"Please, Sophie? I insist."

I hesitate for a minute, arguing with myself over whether I should risk driving all the way home in this mood or just stay with Trisha and her family. I don't really feel like being around people right now, but I also don't feel like driving home and dealing with the crazy holiday traffic in the city. I nod and finally say, "Alright, I'll stay. Thank you."

"Of course. What are best friend's for? Come on—finish your hot chocolate and then I will drive you to my house."

"I'll be fine to drive. I'll just follow you."

"No, *I'm* driving," Trisha says stubbornly, giving me a look that says I better not argue.

"But what about my car?" I ask weakly.

"I'll drive your car. I'll just have one of my brothers drive me back later to pick up my car."

"Are you sure?"

"Absolutely."

I drink the last of my hot chocolate, slide out of the booth, and follow Trisha out to my car. Handing her the keys, I sit down in the passenger seat as she gets into the driver's seat. We make the short drive to her house in silence and she helps me carry my suitcase inside.

Her house is full of noise and chatter as all of her family members are baking cookies, playing games, or singing along to Christmas music. Her young nieces and nephews are chasing each other around the house giggling and screaming. "Sorry about all of the noise," Trisha says.

"It's okay." I give her a half smile. "Maybe all of this cheer will be good for me."

We set my things down next to the couch in the den and I excuse myself to the bathroom so that I can wash my face to make myself at least look presentable before I start interacting with her family. Closing the door behind me, I go to the sink and turn on the cool water. Splashing it over my face, I try to erase the evidence that I have been crying all evening. Glancing into the mirror I see that I look a little better, but not much. "Best it's going to get, I guess," I mumble to myself as I plaster a fake smile onto my face.

I wander into the kitchen to find Trisha snacking on freshly baked cookies. "Here, have a cookie! It'll make you feel better," she says as she holds one out for me.

I take the cookie from her hand and nibble on it

as I say hi and give hugs to the rest of her family. We spent so much time together as children that her family feels like a second family to me. Her brothers and sisters feel like mine and it's comforting to be surrounded by them.

I spend the rest of the night visiting with Trisha's family, joking with her brothers and sisters, reminiscing with her parents, and playing with her nieces and nephews—the whole time pretending like I'm happy and nothing is wrong. There's no need to put a damper on everyone else's fun.

When it's finally time for bed, Trisha walks into the den with me to help pull out the couch bed and put blankets on it. "How are you doing, Sophie?" she asks. "I know all of that in there," she motions to the kitchen and living room, "was just you putting on a brave face."

"I'm doing alright," I lie. "Not great, but I'll live." I hear my voice crack and feel the familiar sting of tears again. "Now that it's quiet, though, I can't help but think about Matt and the disaster that this vacation has turned into."

"You'll be okay, Sophie. I know it hurts, but you'll get through it. Don't let that jerk ruin your whole Christmas."

I smile at her and say, "I'll try. Thanks again for everything."

Trisha gives me a hug before saying goodnight and going to her own room. I close the door to the den, crawl into bed, and turn off the lamp. The memories and the betrayal all flood back to me as I shut my eyes. All I can do is cry myself to sleep.

MATT

Last night was the worst night of my life. After Sophie stormed out of the cabin I just stood there trying to figure out how to fix this mess. A million thoughts had raced through my head, but I hadn't been able to come up with anything. Eventually I had gone to my room and tried to sleep, but I had just tossed and turned all night.

This morning I'm not doing much better either. I'm still pissed at Victoria, but I'm more angry at myself for not coming clean to Sophie in the first place. Sitting around the cabin isn't helping anything. It's just too quiet without Sophie here. I miss her.

Throwing on my jacket and boots I head to my truck to go into town. Maybe a hot chocolate and a walk outside will help to clear my head. At this rate, anything will be better than sitting around here by myself. I can't stand the quiet and emptiness. Thinking about how angry and hurt she was last night is killing me as I walk past Sophie's empty room.

As I pull up in front of the diner and step out of my truck I see Trisha storming towards me, her eyes shooting daggers in my direction. "Matt," she says cooly, crossing her arms. "Why are you such an idiot? Wasn't breaking Sophie's heart once enough for you? You are such an asshole!"

I wince at her words, knowing that they are true. "I deserve that. Have you seen Sophie?" I ask hopefully. "Where is she?"

"Why the hell would I tell you?" Trisha asks angrily.

"Because! I need to talk to her. I need her to let me explain. It was all a huge misunderstanding," I say as I feel the tears building in my eyes.

"A misunderstanding, huh?"

"Yes! That kiss meant nothing. That *woman* means nothing to me! Hell, I never want to see her again. Please, Trisha. You have to believe me and convince Sophie to let me explain," I say desperately.

Trisha raises her eyebrows. "Explain to me first. Then *maybe* I'll tell you where Sophie is."

"I screwed up."

"You think?" she says sarcastically.

"Yes, I know I screwed up. I should have told Sophie right away. That woman—the one who she saw kissing me—is a crazy stalker. I've spent an entire year trying to get away from her. She wants us to be a couple and will do *anything* to get to me."

"Why don't you just get a restraining order?"

"I threatened her with one *now*, but it's tricky. She's my boss's daughter. I've been afraid of losing my job if I did. But yesterday was the last straw and I *will* file for one. She admitted to breaking into my office and my personal desk to find out where I was. She came here to find me. *She* kissed *me*. I shoved her away and told her to get lost—but I'm guessing Sophie didn't stick around long enough to see that part."

Trisha pats my arm and shakes her head sadly. "No, she definitely didn't see that part. She is crushed."

I take a deep breath to push back the tears that

are still threatening. "Please tell me where she is. I need to see her. I need to make this right."

Trisha glances around to think for a minute before her eyes land back on mine. "Alright. I'll help you. *But,* I swear—don't you dare screw it up this time."

"I promise. I'll make things right. I will *never* hurt Sophie again."

"She's staying at my place. Go to the Christmas Eve dance tomorrow night. I'll convince her to go and make sure she gives you a chance to talk to her."

I don't want to wait until tomorrow night to talk to Sophie, but I know that there is no use arguing with Trisha. Besides, if we are at a big public event Sophie won't want to cause a scene and she will listen to me. So maybe Trisha is right to make me wait.

"Okay, I'll go to the dance. Just *please* make sure you get her there. Thanks, Trisha. I owe you."

"You're welcome." She turns to walk away and I'm left standing alone on the sidewalk in front of the diner.

Now that I know Sophie didn't leave town, I feel a little better. I just have to figure out what to say to beg for her forgiveness. Making my way inside I go to the counter to order my drink. "One hot chocolate to go, please."

"Coming right up," the cashier says as she takes my credit card.

A few minutes later with my hot chocolate in hand I exit the diner and start strolling down the main street, wandering aimlessly, to think. I *have* to get Sophie back.

SOPHIE

I wake up in Trisha's den feeling absolutely exhausted. It's a little chilly this morning and the blankets are keeping me warm, but I need to get up. I slowly stretch and finally drag myself out of bed. Going into the bathroom across the hall, I take a look at myself in the mirror. The reflection staring back at me is a complete mess. My hair is carelessly thrown into a messy bun on the top of my head with strands of loose hair flying in every direction. My eyes are red and puffy and my nose looks like Rudolph's thanks to all of my crying. Mascara is smudged all over my cheeks because I didn't care enough last night to wash my makeup off before bed and it ran down in streaks from the tears. I look like I haven't slept in a month.

My heart doesn't hurt any less this morning either. In fact, I think it hurts worse. Letting out a sigh, I grab a washcloth from the towel closet and try to scrub the mascara off of my face the best I can. I yank the ponytail holder out of my hair and quickly run a brush through it. After I brush my teeth I give myself one more look in the mirror, hoping to see someone more put together than I feel. There is nothing I can do about my red puffy eyes, but at least I no longer look like a complete disaster. It will just have to do.

As I walk out into the hallway I hear Trisha coming into the house—back from picking up her car at the diner. "Morning, Sophie," I hear her call as she walks towards me. "Are you feeling any better?"

"No, not really."

"Get dressed and come with me. I have just the thing to cheer you up," Trisha says with a smile.

"What?" I ask suspiciously.

"We're going dress shopping! To get dresses for the dance tomorrow night."

"I'm not going to the dance, Trisha. I'm not in the mood for celebrating."

"Oh come on! You *have* to go! I'm not going to let my best friend sit around and mope over a guy on Christmas Eve—especially when there is a dance going on. Please?" she begs, pouting out her bottom lip.

"Fine. But it won't be any fun. I'll go with you—just stop pouting."

"Yay!" Trisha says excitedly, grabbing my arm and dragging me into the den. "Now hurry up and get dressed! We have some shopping to do." She practically skips out of the room to let me get ready.

Once we are both ready, we hop into Trisha's car and she drives us to Lisa's Formalwear, the local dress shop. As we head inside we can't help but gaze at all of the elegant formal dresses in the window.

"Welcome!" the shop owner says. "What can I help you with today?"

"We are looking for dresses for the Christmas Eve dance tomorrow night," Trisha says.

"Well, you've definitely come to the right place! Take a look around and let me know if you ladies see anything you like."

"Sounds good," I reply as we both nod and start walking around the shop to look through the racks of beautiful gowns. There are gowns in any color you can imagine. Some of them have intricate designs made with beads and crystals while others are more plain and simple. Trisha already has an armful of gowns—both long and short—to try on, but I haven't seen anything that I'm dying to try on yet.

"I can tell you can't wait to play fashion show, Trisha, so why don't you go try those on first and then we can find something for me," I chuckle as I point towards the dressing room.

"Okay! You don't have to tell me twice!" Trisha squeals as she streaks off towards the dressing rooms.

I take a seat on a chair and stare blankly into space while I wait for her to model her first pick. I still don't feel like going to the dance, but Trisha was right about shopping cheering me up a little. This has raised my spirits a little, at least for the time being.

She steps out in her first dress, a short purple one with a lacy design. "Hmm—I'm not sure if I like this one on me. It looked better on the hanger," she says.

"Yeah—it's a little too plain. I don't think it has that wow factor you are usually looking for."

We repeat the process a few more times until she comes out wearing a magnificent dress—a long silver strapless gown with crystal embellishments all over it. "What do you think?" she asks with a giant grin on her face.

"It looks *amazing* on you."

"Thanks! It's perfect! Just what I was looking for. Now—let me change and we'll find *your* perfect dress."

Trisha walks back into her dressing room to change and I wander over to a rack of dresses near the back of the store to search for my gown. The shop owner comes out of a back room carrying a garment bag. "I remembered a specific gown that I just got in and haven't had a chance to put out yet. I think it might be perfect for you," she says as she makes her way over to me.

She unzips the bag and my jaw drops. This gown is the most gorgeous thing I have ever seen! It's a floor length, light blue A-line gown with crystals all along the neckline. The cap sleeves are encrusted with crystals and sparkly beads. The skirt flows out at the bottom and is adorned with silver glittery snowflakes. "It's beautiful," I whisper.

"What's beautiful?" Trisha asks, coming up behind me. "Oh, wow!" she gasps as she sees the gown. "You *have* to try that on!"

Thanking the owner, I take the gown into the dressing room to try it on. It fits perfectly. It hugs me in all of the right places and looks wintery and magical. My eyes fill with tears, but this time they are happy tears. "You were right. I do feel better," I say as I step out to show Trisha. "This dress makes me feel ready to celebrate Christmas and dance the night away."

"You look—incredible. It's like that gown was made for you."

"Thanks. Let me change and then we can shop for accessories," I say with a smile—a genuine one this time.

We spend a good part of the afternoon looking for shoes and jewelry before finally making our purchases. We put our bags into Trisha's car and head to the diner to pick up some treats to bring home to her family.

When we arrive back at her house her family is busy making dinner. "We're back!" Trisha shouts. "And we brought dessert!"

As I watch everyone around me talking and laughing I smile to myself. Today really has been good for me. I'm not going to get over my heartbreak anytime soon, but maybe I can still salvage this Christmas vacation.

MATT

I've been nervous ever since I ran into Trisha yesterday. The anticipation of seeing Sophie at the dance tonight is driving me crazy. A million questions keep running through my head. What if Trisha wasn't able to convince Sophie to come? What if she does come, but bolts as soon as she sees me? What if she hates me so much that she *is* willing to make a scene just so that she doesn't have to listen to me?

If she truly hates me now, well then I deserve to be alone forever. If she doesn't forgive me, I don't think I will ever be able to forgive myself for hurting her again. Sophie is such an amazing, beautiful, loving woman who deserves so much more than a jerk like me. I should just let her go, let her move on, but I'm selfish. She is the best thing that has ever happened in my life and I refuse to lose her without a fight.

After putting on my suit and tie, I head into the bathroom to fix my hair and make sure that I didn't miss any stubble when I shaved this morning. Giving myself one final look in the mirror I tell myself, "You can do this. Let her know how much she means to you." Taking a deep breath, I walk out into the living room to put on my dress shoes. Before heading out to my truck, I grab my gift for Sophie and I walk out the door.

A little while later I arrive at the community center, where the dance is being held, and I park my truck. I sit in silence for a few minutes and pray that Sophie will hear me out. I take a deep breath to calm my nerves before making my way inside.

Walking into the dance hall feels like I have been transported into a beautiful winter wonderland. Blue and white lights shimmer throughout the entire space. Fake trees with their bare branches covered in fake snow line the entrance and the perimeter of the room. Positioned along the sides and bent so that they form an arch over the center of the room are towers of white, silver, and blue balloons. White flickering candles are surrounding the trees and sitting atop the few refreshment tables along the back wall. Glittering white and silver snowflakes hang from the ceiling and the pillars in the corners of the room are wrapped with a combination of white, silver, and blue streamers. It feels almost magical.

Looking around searching for Sophie, it seems like the entire town has already gathered here. My eyes scan the crowd until I finally see her walking through another entrance on the far side with Trisha. My breath catches in my throat, my palms start to sweat, and my jaw drops at how beautiful she looks tonight. The last time I saw her this dressed up was our senior prom. Her gown looks absolutely gorgeous on her. Her hair is pulled to the side, secured over one shoulder with a silver sparkly hair clip. The light hitting the crystals on her dress and in her hair make them sparkle, like hundreds of tiny stars surrounding her. She takes my breath away.

I wait until she has crossed towards the center of the room before making my move—hoping that it will keep her from turning around and sprinting out the door at the sight of me. Her back is to me when I walk up to her and Trisha. I reach out to tap her shoulder, but think better of it and slowly pull my hand back to my side. Clearing my throat I say, "Sophie." Her back stiffens and she doesn't move. "Can we talk, please?"

She still doesn't move or answer. Trisha gently grabs Sophie's hand and says, "You should listen to him for a minute. Give him a chance to explain."

Sophie pulls away from Trisha, giving her an annoyed look, and turns to glare at me. If looks could kill, I'd be dead. I'm terrified that she's going to leave. "Fine," she huffs after a minute. "Let's get this over with." She stomps over to a quiet corner near one of the pillars and I follow. "You have five minutes, Matt, so start talking."

"Sophie—I know I hurt you once when we were teenagers, but you have to believe me that I never meant to hurt you again. That kiss you saw wasn't what it looked like. And that woman means absolutely *nothing* to me."

"Oh, really? She seemed to think so since she called you *my love* and threw herself at you," Sophie answers bitterly.

"She's delusional! Those phone calls I've been receiving were from her. She's a stalker."

"Your stalker?"

"Yes! She has been stalking me for over a year. She's my boss's daughter."

"Why didn't you just tell me when you started receiving those phone calls, Matt?"

"I *should* have told you about her right away, but I didn't want to drag you into my drama. I thought I was protecting you. I came to the cabin to hide from her, but obviously she found me. *She* kissed *me*. If you had stuck around for just a minute longer you would have seen that I pushed her away and told her to get lost. I told her to leave me alone and never contact me again. Even if it costs me my job."

"You did?" she asks.

"Of course I did. I love you, Sophie. I have always loved you and I will never stop loving you. *You* are the only one I have ever wanted."

With tears in her eyes she says, "I love you, too, Matt! Always and forever."

Putting my arms intimately around her waist, I pull her in close to me. I rub a tear away from her cheek with my thumb. Our lips meet in a passionate kiss—the first of our new future together. As we finally pull away, I kiss a few remaining tears from her face. "I've got something for you," I say as I reach into my pocket. Pulling out the wrapped bracelet I picked up at the Christmas village market, I hand it to her. "Open it."

"I'm sorry—I didn't bring your gift. Obviously."

"It's alright. I didn't expect you to after what happened. Just open it."

Sophie rips off the wrapping paper, crumpling it in her hand, revealing the long velvety box. Slowly she opens it. "Oh, wow! Matt—it's—it's beautiful!" she exclaims as she sees the charm bracelet. "I love it!"

"I hoped you would. It reminded me of our snowball fight and the night you decided to give me a second chance."

"It's perfect. Will you help me put it on?"

"Of course." She hands me the bracelet and I gently clasp it around her wrist. Taking her by the hand I lead her out to the dance floor. We sway together slowly to the music, holding each other close. "You are my whole world, Sophie. I don't want to spend another minute without you in my life."

"Don't worry, Matt. I'm not going anywhere." She wraps her arms tighter around my neck and whispers, "You're my whole world too. I love you."

"Love me forever?"

"Forever."

ONE YEAR LATER....

I pace around the living room nervously—holding a little velvet box in my pocket—as I wait for Sophie to finish getting dressed for the Christmas Eve dance. Once again we rented the same cabin that had brought us back together last year. Her parents, and sister Jessica, are staying at the hotel in town and are planning on meeting us at the dance. Sophie had wanted her sister to get dressed over here, but Jessica insisted that it would be better if she just meets us at the community center. Jessica knows what's about to happen—Sophie has no idea.

Hearing Sophie's soft footsteps approaching, I stop pacing and turn to see her walking towards me in a beautiful green satin gown. "You look amazing," I say.

"Thank you. You look quite handsome yourself." She closes the distance between us and wraps her arms around my neck to pull me in for a kiss. "Are you okay, Matt? You're shaking?" she says with a concerned expression on her face.

With a deep, shaky breath, I say, "I'm fine. But there's something I want to do before we head to the dance." Taking her left hand in mine, I drop to one knee. Her free hand flies up to cover her mouth as her eyes widen. "Sophie, one year ago you gave me the best Christmas present ever when you gave me a second chance. You let me back into your life, allowed me to show you how much I truly love you. Last Christmas I told you that I didn't want to spend another minute without you in my life. I still don't want to spend another minute without you. So...," I pull the box out of my pocket and open it—displaying a gorgeous diamond ring, "will you spend the rest of your life with me? Will you marry me?"

"Yes!" she says as tears fill her eyes. "Yes, of course I'll marry you, Matt!"

I slide the ring onto her finger before standing and pulling her into an embrace, kissing her passionately. My dreams have finally come true. I can't wait to spend every Christmas from now on with the woman I love, who will soon be my wife.

THE END

THANK YOU FOR READING!

If you enjoyed this story, please take a second to leave a review on Amazon. I appreciate your support.

Be sure to sign up for my newsletter at https://www.emorie-cole.com
to get details about upcoming projects and access to exclusive content.

UPCOMING RELEASES

New Series from Emorie Cole

Coming Early 2021

Romance in the Keweenaw

Love at the Inn: Wilkins Harbor - Book 1

Be sure to join my social and check out my website for all the latest info about this new series! The Keweenaw is a remote location in the beautiful Upper Peninsula of Michigan.

Emorie Cole

ACKNOWLEDGMENTS

I want to thank my wonderful husband for giving me the support to follow my dreams. Without him, my writing wouldn't be possible. He has been a huge help to me with advertising and website design. He has also been an amazing sounding board for ideas, a helping hand with editing, and isn't afraid to give me critique.

ABOUT THE AUTHOR

Emorie Cole is a small town girl who loves to show her creative side through her writing. She wants her readers to be swept into the world of steamy, small town romances where they'll feel emotional bonds being formed between new loves and second chances.

When she's not writing you can find her curled up with a good book, spending time with her family, playing with her dog, and enjoying the seasons in the beautiful Upper Peninsula of Michigan.

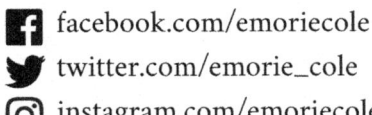

facebook.com/emoriecole
twitter.com/emorie_cole
instagram.com/emoriecole

Made in the USA
Monee, IL
27 October 2021